Distorted

MELODY JONES

For my grandmother,
Irene Gardner - the most amazing person I know.

To my daughters,
Love yourself, be brave, be fearless.

Chapter 1

October, 2009

Lucy

THE COOL LIQUID SLIDES DOWN MY throat. Music thumps in the background. Friends are chatting and dancing in the cool California breeze. My buzz is definitely on, and the cute guys here abound. I make my way between friends, trying to figure out whose house this is. I know we are in a neighborhood belonging to Mission Valley High School – our rivals. My friend, Jenna, is definitely on her way to wasted, so I walk toward where she stands on the other side of the typical California pool – a kidney bean shape, with a hot tub attached at one end. Several large cement areas dotted with lounge chairs flank the sides of the pool. Grass butts up to the concrete, and large urns planted with flowers break up the horizon.

Snatching a bottle of water from the cooler, I hand it to Jenna and tell her to guzzle. She laughs at me, as usual, and rolls her eyes.

"You are going to have to be carried out of this party if you don't mix in some water here and there, lady. We all know what a pain in the ass you are when you are drunk," I laugh.

"You always have my back, Lucy. What would I do without you?" She hugs me, thrusting the entire weight of her body onto mine. We laugh as we almost fall to the ground.

"Let's dance!" Jenna shouts, grabbing my hand and pulling me toward the makeshift dance floor. I keep catching the cute guy with the sandy blonde hair looking at me from across the pool. He is so hot – he probably has a girlfriend.

"Don't Cha" by The Pussycat Dolls starts playing through the Bluetooth speakers surrounding the backyard, and all the girls at the party go crazy. Most of them quickly gather to partake in the short dance. My face hurts from laughing and smiling. My heavy breathing from dancing can't appear attractive, so I leave the dance floor in search of a drink. Spying a cooler on the other side the yard, I walk over hoping to find a water or soda.

"Can I get you something to drink?" is spoken in a deep, rich voice from behind me.

I turn and see the guy that has been watching me. Looking over my shoulder to see who he is talking to, I realize I am the only person around. Stunned, I turn back toward him. He is still there, looking at me.

"Thanks," I say as he holds out a bottled water.

"I'm Grayson," he says.

Silence. And more silence.

"What's your name?" Grayson asks me, while I stand there staring at his defined chest, displayed generously in a tight white t-shirt.

"I'm Lucy," stumbles awkwardly from my lips.

We talk about what schools we attend, sports, parties, and cars. He loves cars like I do. I'm a Ford girl, but he is definitely a Chevy guy. I can picture him behind the wheel of an enormous truck – you know, the kind of truck always driven by hot guys. They have big wheels and shiny chrome bumpers and exhaust you can hear for miles.

I excuse myself to pee because I'm on the verge of having an accident. I catch my friends on the way to the bathroom, and we make a group trip. With the door closed, Jenna, Taylor, and Kendall grill me about Grayson. They all saw me talking to him and want to know where he came from and if his eyes are as beautiful up close as they from far away. I tell them the little bit I have learned and that, yes, his eyes are as stunning as they imagined.

We each have our turn to tinkle, wash our hands, fix our make-up, and fluff or flatten our hair. Then we make our way out back, the girls in search of fun, and me in search of Grayson. I find him out by the pool talking with a bunch of good looking, athletic guys. He waves me over to him.

Grayson walks away from his buddies toward me, handing me a fresh beer. We pick up where we left off in our conversation. There is an ease to our chatter, like we are old friends. I can't help getting caught staring into his large, hazel eyes, or admiring the muscles straining against his shirt sleeves. The party carries on with lots of dancing, girls screaming, and guys tossing footballs. Grayson and I make the rounds, talking up my friends, doing a little slow dance. He takes good care of me, keeping me constantly supplied with a fresh beer or a bottle of water, escorting me to the bathroom, and talking with my crazy friends. The night is like a dream.

My head is pounding despite the silence of the room. It takes several minutes to get my bearings before I flop my legs over the side of the sofa and realize I'm tethered to the floor. Fear grips my heart as I try to recall where I am, how I got here, who did this to me.

The door opens harshly. Fluorescent lights flicker above me. I'm overcome with the smell of noodles cooking. A large, imposing figure is standing before me. A black hood disguises his face.

Looking down, I realize I'm wearing nothing but my underwear. Tears flood my cheeks. Screams erupt from my lips. My heart races. Then nothing. The light switches off, and I'm left in total darkness.

Chapter 2

"LUCY, YOU HAVE BEEN COMING TO SEE me for almost two years. We have made incredible progress, and you have become an amazing young woman. But when are we going to really dig in and fix your way of thinking?"

"What do you mean?" I ask, as though I have no idea to what Andrea, my therapist, is referring.

"Don't play coy, Lucy. You avoid discussing your weight every time I bring up the matter."

Silence ensues as Andrea waits for my answer. We play this game once in a while. Andrea asks me a question I don't want to answer, and we sit in silence, staring at each other, until I cave in and say something.

Andrea's office is in her home – a charming mansion on the outskirts of Griffith Park in Los Angeles. There are bookshelves surrounding the large picture window which overlooks her sloping garden. The trickling sound of water from a large wall fountain seeps through the glass panes of the window. The lighting is low, warmed by the flicker of a candle. Andrea searches through her box of gemstones for some type of comfort to prepare for our session. During our appointments she holds each rock, rubbing them between her palms. Sometimes she chooses several stones to occupy her hands at once. I always ask what she is looking for in that box, and she usually says she is searching for inspiration. I know those rocks are all different colors and substances with particular meanings, but I never look them up, for fear of what I may discover. Maybe I choose not to know. She rubs the smooth stone between her hands and resumes staring at me, waiting for my answer. A mutual stare down occurs until she gives in and tells me that today she chose yellow jasper, a form of quartz believed to aid in channeling positive energy and easing worry.

"What's wrong with my weight?" I say, knowing this will annoy her.

"Nothing is wrong with your weight, but I know how you feel about it. It makes you uncomfortable, self-conscious. You use it as a crutch to keep people away from you. It's an excuse to hide from life, an excuse for anything that doesn't go your way. You deserve so much more than you allow yourself. When are you going to take a chance on yourself, Lucy?"

I was ripped from my comfortable existence and thrown into a tunnel of despair. I lost years of my life from the aftermath of that incident, hoping each morning

I would wake and want to live, want to love again. Years I should have been having fun with my friends, going to college, joining a sorority – instead I was isolated and alone, my friends too busy with their own lives to hang out with a loser like me. My family watched me wallow in a swamp of despair and did nothing outside of sending me to the hospital for a month. I needed my family, my friends. I needed somebody to see me, believe in me. It was through that experience I realized the only person I can rely on is myself. I spent years trying to find myself, years that I will never get back. "I cannot, and will not, risk that happening again!" I huff, tears plummeting from my eyes and spotting my crisp, white shirt.

"So what am I supposed to do? Tell me how to trust again, trust others enough to let them get close to me. How?" I yell, my arms flailing in frustration and despair. "I'm not worth anyone's effort," I whisper.

"Lucy, you are worth so much more than you allow yourself. Part of living is learning from the past, trusting the future, and putting yourself out there again. Take baby steps or giant steps, just start taking steps for you. You are amazing. You are strong. You are worthy of love."

"I'm not worthy!" I holler. "Even my own parents don't think I have value. I'm not smart enough, just like my dad says every time I fail to turn a potential client. 'You're not a go-getter, so how will you be successful?' he says."

Andrea sighs loudly, her hand rubbing the yellow jasper. She smiles and digs through her little box of rocks. She pulls out a small stone, the color of apricot, and hands it to me.

"Citrine. It helps clear the mind. It's comforting," she says, watching me inspect the stone that is about the size of a peanut butter cup.

"Prove yourself wrong. Prove that you are worthy. Show me your greatness. You are smart and compassionate- a survivor. The world is at your fingertips. Let's take a chance together, Lucy." Silence ensues. The trickling sound of the fountain buzzes through my brain as my heart thumps violently in my chest.

"I'm scared, Andrea."

"I know you are, but you can do this. You are brave, and you deserve a life beyond your past, beyond your job."

"How do I start? What do I do?"

"I've been reading about alternative therapies related to overcoming abandonment, anxiety, self- esteem, and body dysmorphia. While not a proven therapy, improvement has been shown in patients who were tracked."

"What do I have to do?"

"The therapy requires that you submit to another person."

"What does that even mean? Are talking about being dominant or submissive in sex? You want me to go have sex with some stranger who likes to control women? No way. No."

"I assure you, this isn't about sex. You will not even be required to be naked. I can't ethically recommend this type of therapy, so I'm just going to give you a business card. I'm not going to persuade you to call or participate. This is your choice."

I take the card and stare at the black, glossy paper that

has nothing on it but a phone number and an address.

"Our time is up today, Lucy. Think about our session and decide if you are ready to take back your life. See you next week," Andrea says before she stands and holds her arms out for me to hug her.

Andrea is the only person in my life who hugs me. I asked her once why she does, and she said, "Because you need it."

I get in my Mustang and turn the key, waiting that split second before the growl of the engine drowns out the noise around me. I release the clutch and coast down the hill into the outskirts of Hollywood. I make my way east on Franklin toward the freeway, catching the tail end of rush hour traffic. My head bobs back and forth as I work my way through the stop-and-go traffic and into the valley – my home.

Pulling into the garage of my California bungalow, I switch off my car and hit the button to close the garage door. I quietly make my way through the small garden to the little porch surrounding my back door.

Opening then closing the door, I walk into the bedroom and change into my favorite pajamas. Another night home alone. Another night safe from harm. Another night I will lay awake and wonder, why me? Why did I have to be kidnapped? Why have I had to suffer through these years of depression? Tonight, I will consider change as I stare at the business card crumpled in my fist.

Chapter 3

A PILE OF CHEWED BUBBLE GUM RESTS ON my desk disguised as a volcano of sorts. You know those big gumballs you see in stores all lined up in a rainbow of colors just waiting to become over-the-top party favors? I'm addicted to them. I bite through the sugary coating, and then slowly chew and chew the last bit of sugar from the gum, relishing the jolt of energy to my brain. I place another chewed blob onto the napkin that is hidden from view on my desk. That blob is instantly replaced in my mouth by a fresh ball of goodness. The miniature gum-volcano hiding on my desk continues to grow as I repeat this scenario until my jaw stings from the effort. Wrapping the volcano in a bunch of other trash, I place it in my waste basket, hoping it won't be discovered by anyone in my office.

The offices of First SoCal Bank's *Investment Banking*

Division, where I work as a junior associate, are quite possibly the most conservative work environment on the planet, or at least in the greater Los Angeles area. My work wardrobe consists entirely of navy and black skirt-suits. A plain and simple shell worn underneath my jacket is the only option for a little variety. However, getting too daring with that pop of color can earn some curious looks from the older folks in the bank offices. Pant suits on women are considered acceptable only for casual Friday attire. Any meetings with potential or existing clients must be had wearing a conservative skirt-suit.

I don't mind the environment so much. Blending into the group is my modus operandi after all. So I find other ways to be discreetly rebellious – such as hiding my gum volcano on top of my desk. I also keep an assortment of glittery, but professional, pens on my desk, so when I need to take notes or make a list of things to do, I can do it with a little flair.

This is not the career I had envisioned for myself. While working on a project for a finance class in college, I met a nice man who was mentoring students in the business program. He liked my work and suggested I submit a resumé for a summer internship program at First SoCal Bank. Not believing I would ever be chosen to work for a prominent financial services company, I submitted my resumé, completely prepared for rejection.

To my shock, I was chosen for the program. Then, upon graduation, I was invited to join the company as an assistant to a junior associate. I took the job, frankly because it was good money. I already knew many of the associates, so the opportunity felt comfortable and didn't scare the hell out of me. It was the easy way out, even though I knew it would only be a matter of time before I was fired or transferred to another department, because finance is simply not my thing. I loathe financial calculations, statistics, and all those forms of math that are required to get a business degree from a polytechnic college. I enrolled at Cal Poly to study marketing, which I thought a great fit for me at the time. And it is. I love the process of evaluating a brand for new opportunities, studying trends, and trying to forecast how markets are changing or growing. Plus, the vast majority of classes at Cal Poly were available to take online, something that was appealing to me back then.

After the kidnapping, my mom helped me, through home schooling, finish my senior classes so I could graduate high school on time. I was personally struggling to deal with the reality of *the incident* and, in the process, had retreated from my friends, school, family, everything. After a few months of kicking around the house, I grew restless, despite my continued depression and despair. I looked into a variety of education programs and ultimately chose Cal Poly because it was close to home and had a large presence of off-campus students- students who commuted to school, just as I would. Nobody in my on-campus classes knew me, so I didn't feel threatened in any way and was largely seen but not heard. I struggled through the math portion of the curriculum, but I finally came to an understanding with Math that we could get along, though we would never be friends. Funny that a job I love happens to involve studying figures and ratios, which I despise.

Three years later, I'm still here at First SoCal and remain perpetually surprised that I'm pretty good at this finance stuff. Being promoted to junior associate last year was amazing, but terrifying, because I have a secret: I am horrible at cold-calling and selling clients my ideas. While I seem to be meeting my sales targets, every month when the report comes out, I panic. My hands become clammy, and I scratch my skin until it bleeds. I'm waiting for the day I will get fired for non-performance. Stupid, I know. But the entirety of my late teenage and early adult years were filled with failures, disappointing my parents in every way possible. Being forcefully hospitalized for depression only added to the disappointment I caused my parents. Mind you, my hospitalization was indirectly caused by my parents because of what happened to me seven years ago. The kidnapping was related to my father's business, and I was the easiest target.

Before my mind drifts into that darkness, I grab another gumball and finish the proposal that I will be presenting next week. I need this commission and the security it will bring. The funds from this commission will secure my mortgage another month, my bills another month, my life another month. I have nowhere to go if I am unsuccessful at this job, if I fail to take care of myself. My grandparents are gone, leaving my mother as the only real family in my life. An unhealthy fear of being homeless or carless drives me to make those anxiety-inducing sales calls. From an early age, it has been apparent to me: take care of yourself, because nobody else is going to do it for you.

My parents divorced during my middle school years,

and I handled it as expected – with fear and rebellion. Somehow though, I managed to stay in the good graces of my teachers and my parents. Mom supported me during this trying time but was largely absent, doing her best to navigate a new life for which she had not prepared. Dad was consumed with work, growing his business, and dating more women than I could comprehend. I love my dad, but we just don't understand one other. Actually, he doesn't seem to understand women in general, and I can't fathom how he could allow his daughter to suffer in silence. My parents have always disapproved of anyone creating a spectacle or bringing drama to the family- their definition of which would be anything that is a pain in the ass, costs money, or could be frowned upon by others. My devastating case of depression after the kidnapping was largely ignored by them. Sure, they sent me to a therapist and complained about the expense of my sessions, but they otherwise avoided discussing the situation. It was as though saving me brought them no joy. Years later, I could see that their provision of these therapy sessions wasn't really about saving my life, saving me from depression. It was about my parents maintaining the appearance of doing what was expected. They helped their freakish daughter by sending her to therapy. What else could they do? I try not to get angry about it, but I often fail. I know that I would give all I have, sacrifice everything possible, so that my child never has to feel what I felt. Sure, as time passed, my depression improved. I still have moments where I fall into the darkness, but Andrea, my therapist, helps me understand and move forward.

My colleague, Beau, has been blowing up my messaging inbox with a bunch of nonsense about upcoming appointments and proposals we are jointly working. Beau is my closest friend at the bank, and we also happen to work well together. His strength is reaching out to potential clients, while I am skilled at preparing proposals and finding the best financing to fit our clients' needs. We make a productive team.

Beau: *throw away that volcano*
Beau:*lunch*
Beau:*10 minutes*
Me:*I hate your rapid fire messages…*
Beau:*lunch*
Me:*I'm not eating*
Beau:*chicken shop?*
Me:*see you in 10*

We are like a brother and sister pair who are actually fond of one another. It also helps that Beau is hot as fuck. Seriously. The make-your-panties-wet kind of hot. Sandy blonde hair kept neatly trimmed, a well-proportioned face, and the most stunning hazel eyes on this planet. I would be lying if I said I didn't daydream about what it would be like to date someone like Beau. Or have mind-blowing sex with him. I can't even begin to imagine just how astounding the sex would be, but I am certain it would be the fuck of my life.

I haven't dated anyone since high school, and I don't

consider short term boyfriends to be a good example of what adult dating is really like anyway. It has been three years since I've had sex, and before that, it was four years. I call myself a born-again virgin. It's not that I don't like sex. It's just that I hadn't had much sexual experience before *the incident* changed the course of my life. And since then, it has taken everything I have, everything I am, to keep myself alive. Sex has been on the backburner, and I have had no problem leaving it there to simmer. Plus, I would have had to meet a guy in order to have sex, but it has taken me years to begin trusting people again.

Beau: I'm waiting

Me: oops, on my way

Beau: you're buying

Me: fine

I grab my purse and turn for the stairs – my exercise for the day – making my way down the five flights to find Beau standing at the bottom waiting for me.

"What took you so long?" he says, slightly annoyed.

"I got distracted. Let's go. I'm driving," I say, turning toward the exit.

Beau doesn't object when I say I'm driving, because he knows it's a battle he won't win. I grew up in Southern California, and if I inherited one thing from my dad, it is my fondness for muscle cars. I'm not sure how Beau got such poor taste in vehicles, but he seriously needs my help. He drives a Volkswagen Passat of all thing—a chick's car, through and through. Every time you see a Passat passing by, sure enough, there is a female behind the wheel. A man as hot as Beau driving this type of car is not something my mind can grasp. He claims it's a reliable German car, suitable for chauffeuring clients. I say it's a boring person's car, and he's not that person. To this, he usually just rolls his eyes and changes the subject.

We settle into the plush leather seats of my Mustang and drive to my favorite mom-and-pop food joint, The Chicken King. I don't know what it is about these little takeout huts which dot the landscape of SoCal, but each one is distinctive in its own greasy and amazing way. Most of the modest restaurants are operated by families of Greek heritage, and The Chicken King is no different. Walking into the well-worn eatery, I am overwhelmed by the scent of fresh herbs and succulent, roasting chickens that have been rubbed with fresh garlic and a variety of other spices. The owner greets us with a hearty hello and makes small talk with Beau about something sports-related. I tune out briefly as I continue to inhale the mouthwatering aromas that envelop me.

I order my usual—roasted chicken breast with hummus and eggplant on the side. Beau consistently gets the same ultra-healthy meal of double chicken breasts and plain vegetables. I have never seen Beau without a shirt, but I am confident he is hiding some amazing abs under his tailored suit.

Grabbing our trays, we find a small booth in the corner near the front door. The melamine bench creeks as I sit down, and the table rests against the belt on my skirt, reminding me of my swollen belly. I chastise myself that I should have ordered the steamed vegetables.

Beau's phone chirps constantly throughout our meal,

yet he barely gives it a glance, despite my assurance that it won't offend me if he needs to pick-up the messages.

He says it's not important—just some girl who won't leave him alone—and then he starts chatting about golf. Why he insists on talking golf with me, I will never know. I've come to the understanding that I can just stare aimlessly at his pouty lips while he talks, without worrying about missing important details of the conversation, because he knows I don't play golf and really couldn't care less about anything he is saying.

As we finish our lunches, Beau starts in on me about one of our upcoming appointments. He has a bit of a Jekyll-and-Hyde disposition. Despite him being younger than me, he occasionally treats me like a child. It doesn't usually bother me, however, because I know it's just part of his personality.

"Lucy, do you have all the financing details and their accompanying analysis ironed out yet? Usually you are one step in front of me on these things, but I needed them last week, and I still haven't received them," he says, his voice filled with annoyance.

"I sent them to you a few days ago."

"Well, obviously I didn't get them, because I'm asking you for them now."

"I'll resend them to you first thing when I get back to the office," I say, deflated.

"It isn't like you to be sloppy like this. Should I continue to expect this lack of attention-to-detail from you? Because if that's the case, I may need to refrain from partnering with you in the future."

Beau has never threatened me like this before. The fact is, I do all the important financing work on these deals. He is simply a better spokesperson and salesman than I am.

Finishing our meals, we empty our trays into the trash bin and ride home, while Beau chatters about the latest girl who is pursuing him, and I pretend to be interested.

Parting ways with Beau in the lobby, I take the stairs to my office on the 5th floor to resend him the missing files. I stow my bag behind my desk and pull open my gumball drawer. Positioned neatly in the center of the gumball pile is a quick-prep container of Mac Made Easy.

My heart thunders in my chest, and my breath becomes short. I can smell the cheese dust inside the container, surrounding me, suffocating me. I feel as though the walls are closing in, and I'm being transported back to that time- that time I was fed nothing but Mac Made Easy for days on end.

I look around to see if there is anyone in our office who doesn't belong here. But the office is mostly empty, as it is still the lunch hour.

I feel panic settling in. I should call downstairs and report this as a breach of security.

But what exactly would I tell them? This container of Mac Made Easy mysteriously ending up in my drawer is not something most people will understand, which means I would have to explain why I'm so panicked. I don't know that I'm ready or willing to reveal information about *the incident* to my employer.

What if it changes how they view my part in this organization? What if it affects my job? What if the company uses it as a means to request my resignation due to the unwelcome security threats and negative attention it may garner?

I could call the FBI, but I feel stupid.

"Hey, Mr. FBI Man. There is a suspicious container of Mac Made Easy in my desk drawer. Can you please call out your tactical team to rescue me?"

What if this is just a coincidence? What if it's really nothing? My mind is reeling with possibilities.

I walk back to my office and stare into the drawer containing the offensive food, trying to decide what to do next. Ultimately, I grab a tissue to cover my hand and carefully remove the container of Mac Made Easy from the drawer, dropping it with a thud into my waste bin.

The decision has been made. I will not report this incident to security or the authorities because I can't be sure it really means anything sinister. I take long, deep breaths, hoping to calm my nerves and settle the uneasiness lingering in my belly.

The smell of processed macaroni and cheese lingers in my nose for the remainder of the afternoon, but I finally manage to push the unnerving event aside and get some work done. Thankfully, my friends help to distract me with their weird texts.

Beau: *This chick doesn't want to go out with me. What do I do?*

Me: *leave her alone*

Beau: *but I want her*

Me: *she doesn't want u*

Beau: *but she has a tight ass*

Me: *don't care. I'm working*

It's just like Beau to insult me at lunch, then ask me for advice about a girl not an hour later.

The next message is from my best friend, Quinn.

Quinn: *how much does a can of chicken soup cost?*

Quinn works out of her apartment. She is a bit of hermit, so we get along great. I spend many evenings with her, drinking cheap wine and binge-watching television shows.

Me: *no idea*

Quinn: *too slow, I didn't virtually win anyway*

Me: *Price is Right?*

Quinn: *Supermarket Scramble*

Me: *I work, remember?*

Quinn: *So do I*

Me: *talk later…working*

I decide to turn off my phone so I will no longer be distracted from my work. The last hour on the clock clicks by slower than a sloth crossing the street.

Driving home, I consider the challenge Andrea has presented me. The entire idea gives me anxiety, but I need to grow up and push myself to understand the fears that consume me. I can't spend the rest of my life watching TV with Quinn or hanging out alone at home. I have permitted my fears to control my life. Maybe there was a time when that was for the best, but now, I'm weary. I don't know who would love me or want me. But maybe I'm ready to put myself out there. Just a little.

I allow the echo of the growling engine to encompass me as I pull into the otherwise silent garage. Shutting down the motor and removing the car key, I hit the button to close the overhead garage door. I carefully make my way out into the yard and toward the back door of my California bungalow. I flip the lock on the deadbolt and close the door on another day.

Chapter 4

Keegan

I'VE BEEN BACK IN SOCAL FOR ALMOST A YEAR, but I still feel like an outsider. Maybe it's because I still have unpacked boxes in my closet and a bunch of random furniture that doesn't really fit in my condo. My awesome, gigantic, leather sofa is so big, it takes up the space that's meant for a dining table in addition to its own designated area in the living room. For the most part, I stand in the kitchen to eat when I'm home, or just chow in front of the television. My buddies don't mind my furnishings because their places are no better. And I've been so busy lately, I haven't seen anyone outside of work anyway. My bedroom furniture is mostly mismatched, but I do have a nice, new, king-size bed, which is all that really matters. Not that I have time to bring home chicks to give it some mileage, but it's ready to go if and when I need it.

Working for the FBI since graduating college, I have been all over the U.S. investigating various crimes, never putting down roots for more than a year at a time. Eight years of fairly constant travel had begun to wear on me, so I decided to return to my home state to be near my parents and family members and the few close friends with whom I have kept in contact.

My parents are still married, and my sister lives in the area as well. Dad is a carpenter for the movie studios. He builds sets on the backlots or pieces that will be taken and used for off-site shoots. Mom is a school teacher, so she had summers free to spend full time with us when we were young. She is a patient lady who dreamt of teaching elementary school when she was a child. Teaching was always enough for her, and it's pleasing to know that my mom made her childhood dreams a reality.

I had an idyllic upbringing in Southern California. I played soccer and baseball when I was young. My dad took me camping for a week every summer at the lakes in the northern part of the state. Every week during the summer, my mom drove us and our friends to the beach. We would body surf and horse around in the sand and salty waves from morning until evening. I don't know how she spent all day watching us kids, but I'm grateful that she did. My sister, Kendra, followed in mom's footsteps and became a teacher as well. She tells me all the funny stories of her middle school students and their complaints about learning math. And there are endless stories of the parents who can't stand the *new math*, as they call it. We have a close, friendly relationship. In many ways, I suppose my returning to California wasn't merely for my parents' sakes, but for mine, for I long to renew my relationship with them as they grow older.

My latest case involves kidnapping, murder-for-hire, and financial crimes. The victim is unaware of the threats to her life. I have been tasked with her surveillance, utilizing a hobby that I had previously kept quiet from my direct command, friends, and family.

Back in college, I studied psychology and criminology. In doing so, my interest in the power and positivity of portraying a dominant in relationships was piqued. Of course, there is a gratifying sexual release that accompanies those individuals who are liberated by domination. I'm no different, but that isn't what drives me to dominate. From a personal standpoint, I enjoy that my actions empower certain types of women who are otherwise vulnerable in their lives.

During those periods of my life when I was single, I would practice my scenes with willing women at BDSM clubs. My partners were always sexually confident women, but I started to notice that the women who had flawed views of themselves really required more of my time, effort, and concentration in order to bring them pleasure. I started to consider this type of a girl a challenge. I did not just seek to satisfy them sexually. I found that I wanted to help them see that their distorted views of themselves were incorrect, and those views did not define their worth. It seemed as though these women joined this type of club not just for the sexual gratification, but to feel wanted, desired. Several of the girls I had longer club relationships with had little to no sexual or social life outside the clubs. I discovered dozens of reasons why the girls had ended up with such views of themselves, and they were varied. Some had low self-esteem. Others had been bullied for reasons associated with their appearance. And still others, over time, had created an unattainable vision of themselves in their minds. Visions of resembling the models on the front of fashion magazine standards – completely irrational. At the end of the day, I wasn't in a place to personally save these girls. I was just a young, inexperienced guy at the time, and I wasn't mature enough to make a real difference in their lives. So I did my best to help them see in themselves what I saw—beautiful women with stories and heartbreak, but with normal, healthy wants and desires.

In the BDSM lifestyle, I am not considered a true dominant. I call myself a failure in that regard because I discovered that I did not want to fully commit my partners into submission. I wanted to give my partners power of body and mind, without taking the last bits of strength from their will. True dominants employ many toys for restraint of their partners, while I enjoy some mild restraints for my partners, I have never desired to use a spanking bench, shackles or any of the various tying techniques employed in BDSM. My greatest tool is helping my partners see their beauty, through speech, touch, skin to skin contact, and acceptance of themselves. Every woman should feel worshipped by her partner, both mentally and physically – a task more difficult than would expect.

At yesterday's roundtable for this latest case, it was suggested that an agent would be needed to go undercover and befriend the victim in our investigation to ensure her safety. The victim has been referred by her therapist to a club that caters to sexual empowerment, which would provide us with an easy way to get another agent undercover to work on this case. Unfortunately, the Bureau doesn't hold classes on BDSM, dominant relationships, or any specialized sexual knowledge when it comes to victims. Knowing I could add valuable expertise to this case, I raised my hand and explained my hobby. My colleagues were initially stunned into silence by my confession. But that silence was quickly followed by jokes about me chaining up my conquests or spanking, and all those other jokes typically made by people who have not studied the specialty.

In the end, my command agreed to assign me to that part of the case. Continuing my review of the case file, it is obvious that Lucy, my assignment, may be my toughest partner yet. She is tightly wrapped up in what happened to her in the past, keeping her protective armor firmly in place. This will be the first time my partner is unaware of how I'm going to help her. I can't help but wonder if I will cause her to break or bloom.

Chapter 5

Lucy

WITHOUT THINKING, I CALL THE number on the business card and make an appointment for my first alternative therapy session. I'm not sure if it's luck, but there is an available appointment this evening. I agree before I change my mind.

Driving into the valley, I'm overcome with fear, the butterflies in my stomach raising my vomit level to a nine. A drop of sweat rolls down the side of my neck. I feel the color drain from my cheeks with each turn of the odometer. What am I thinking? Can I do this?

Checking the address on the card, I pull into the parking lot of a nondescript building – one of the dreary 1960's multiplex offices that can be found by the dozens in this part of the valley. I wouldn't call this area seedy, but

I've definitely been to nicer parts of Los Angeles where the rent was affordable. Ignoring the alarm bells ringing in my brain, I find the building directory on the front wall, locate the suite number, then make my way up the concrete staircase and open the door to a small, plush waiting room. I hear the door chimes, followed by the sound of a door in the rear opening and closing. The faint scent of jasmine and cedar tickles my nose as the jazz music playing in the background calms my nerves.

A woman about fifty years old with porcelain skin and beautiful, silky, black hair quietly walks in and says hello. "You will need to sign these forms. Please be sure to read them thoroughly. When you are done, I will collect you and deliver you to your room."

"Ok, thank you," I say hesitantly. I take the clipboard and sit down on the oversized sofa. The forms are fairly straightforward: A non-disclosure and confidentiality agreement and a liability waiver.

I stand and return the clipboard to the woman who quietly sits behind a sleek glass desk. She checks each page for signatures carefully, then stands and motions me down the hall.

"Please follow me," she says.

We swiftly make our way down the hall to a door marked with a 5 and enter the dimly lit room.

"Please sit in the small chair. Master will be with you when you are ready," she says, then closes the door behind me.

Placing my purse on the table next to the door, I search through it, looking for the stone Andrea gave me after our last therapy session. She would only tell me the name: agate, the fire stone. I need to look this up later and see what powers Andrea thinks I needed for this adventure. Gripping the smooth stone in my hand, I take a deep breath then walk quietly to the designated chair in the seating area.

The room is painted chalky white. The wood floors are a dark, distressed walnut. An oversized sofa covered in the most opulent white I have ever seen creates a conversation area in the middle of the room. Lavish faux fur throws the color of a snow leopard are draped across the back of the sofa. A large, round leather tray lies in the middle of the light grey tufted ottoman. A mismatched collection of hand-poured candles flicker in the dim light, casting shadows around the room.

Again, the smell of jasmine heightens my senses while the sound of trickling water settles the butterflies raging in my belly. There are various mirrors and artwork adorning the walls of the room. The far wall is covered in enormous watercolor of a woman.

My heart is racing with fear and excitement, but my mind is serene. I sink into the plush leather chair, my hands wringing themselves as I wait for my partner to enter. Curious as to what this meeting could entail, I have spent some time researching this type of therapy, exploring dominant and submissive techniques online. I trust Andrea's judgement, so when I saw some of the activities that popped up in my search, I reminded myself that some of the scenes and suggestions must be expert level or whatever. The appointment was described to me as touching therapy, similar to a massage with other psychological components added in accordance with my comfort level and responses. Honestly, I'm not exactly sure what all that means or how it relates to components of BDSM, but I'm here and willing to give Andrea's suggestion a try, because at this point I'm willing to try just about anything to regain control of my life.

The changing vibe of the background music is the only signal of time passing. Crossing and uncrossing my ankles becomes habit. I begin to wonder what I'm doing here when I feel the presence of someone in the room.

Before I can turn to look, a firm, yet suave voice speaks, "Do not turn around Lucy. Your eyes will remain forward, trained on the art before you."

I stare at the wall-sized watercolor of a naked woman. The canvas is mounted to a solid black frame, emphasizing the stark contrasts of the work. The woman appears tranquil, loved, cherished – her depiction merely from the careful brushstrokes of the artist.

The lights dim to a level just above darkness. Fear travels from my belly into my throat. I try to swallow down the lump, but it lingers.

"There is nothing to fear, Lucy. I'm here to help you, but in turn, you will need to agree to my demands. Moving forward, you will only speak if asked a question or given permission. Do you agree?"

"Yes," I whisper.

"These are my conditions:

You will address me as Master.

Eyes will remain forward unless given permission to look elsewhere.

You are expected to do what I ask without hesitation.

What is your favorite candy?"

"Gumballs."

"Your safe word is Gumball. If at any time you are truly fearful, upon utterance of your safe word, I will stop. Do you agree with my conditions?"

"I agree." What did I just agree to? Why am I trusting this person? I need to get out of here.

"Lucy, you are safe with me. We will work together to find you a life worth living, a life worth trusting. But most importantly, we will light the fire in your heart so that it burns brightly, too brilliant to ever fade."

I want to scream, "How can I do that?" but I keep reminding myself not to speak.

"You doubt yourself now, but I promise, change is on the way. Now take off your shoes and lie down on the chaise, eyes facing the canvas."

Slowly removing my shoes and standing, I quietly step to the chaise and lie down, careful to keep my eyes focused on the canvas before me. Goosebumps erupt across my skin, heat blossoms in my core, and fear remains in my thoughts.

Minutes pass before I feel his presence behind me. The rich, thick scent of tobacco and something woody tickles my nose. The butterflies in my belly are fluttering again as I wonder what will happen next.

"I have two final conditions for you. You must not have a sexual relationship with anyone while we are working together. You will leave your cell phone number on the notepad next to the door before you leave. Do you agree?"

"Yes, I think so."

"That is not good enough. You will answer yes or no."

"Yes."

"Honest and prompt responses are essential for our work together to be meaningful. Do you understand?"

"Yes."

"When the lights raise, you are free to leave."

"Is this it? Are we done?"

My question is answered with silence. The lights are raised, and I look around wondering who my Master really is. Confusion suffocates my brain as I try to understand what I'm doing here. Andrea told me to trust her, to trust the process, and to trust myself. But I can't help wanting to run away and never return, to continue to hide in my safe little world of work and my home - keeping my heart safe - holding disappointment at bay by controlling everything in my life.

Grabbing my bag from the table, I jot down my mobile number, open the door, and walk outside to find darkness has cloaked the city, as the warm Santa Ana winds transport fallen leaves across the parking lot. I can't help but feel as though someone is watching. I stop and look around me at the surrounding area and don't see anything suspicious. Maybe I'm just weirded-out by my therapy session.

Sliding down into the cool leather seats of my Mustang, I crank the engine, waiting for its rumbling sound to comfort me.

My brain is crowded with conflicting thoughts of excitement, fear, doubt, and curiosity.

The ding of a text message startles me from my

thoughts. Picking up the phone I see an unknown number.

Unknown: *Stop doubting yourself, Lucy. Always wear stiletto heels for our meetings.*

Unknown: *See you in 2 days. Same time, same place*

I'm just a big ball of doubt. How could he know that I'm full of skepticism and reluctance, as I didn't speak more than ten words during our brief session? And what the heck am I doing seeking professional help at a BDSM club? All things I must discuss with Andrea at my next appointment.

I release the clutch. Maneuvering the Mustang into the steady flow of cars, I make my way back to the freeway. The evening traffic has begun to disperse, so the drive is tolerable. As I zigzag my way between lanes, I notice the car in my rear view mirror seems to be duplicating my every move. Changing lanes quickly and veering off the freeway, I watch in horror as the vehicle mimics my movement and exits the freeway as well. I was so lost in thought, I did not notice the car following me until now. Why is someone tailing me? Did I cut him off, and now I'm being chased by a driver with a case of road rage?

I can't hear anything over the sound of my heart pounding in my chest. The traffic signal at the bottom of the off-ramp is a stale green, so I downshift into third gear and hit the gas as the signal turns yellow. Glancing in the rearview mirror, I see the other car has sped through the light behind me.

The frontage road before me is dark and deserted, but I know there is a large block of apartments and condominiums to the west.

Watching the vehicle behind increase its distance, I press the accelerator hard to the next traffic signal, never making a full stop at the red light. I make a quick right turn and squeeze into the gated condo complex behind a resident. I cut my lights and hope my tail missed my turn. Hurriedly parking in a resident spot, I kill the engine and hunch down into the seat, trying to become invisible.

Minutes tick by without another vehicle or person appearing. Tilting up my head, I peer over the car next to me and see the security gate is clear with no vehicles waiting to enter the parking lot. Maybe this was just a coincidence? Maybe this craziness is just in my mind and not real?

Cranking the engine once again, I pull out onto the street and start making my way home. With just a few blocks left before my street, a sedan comes out of nowhere and rides my rear bumper. My foot hammers the gas pedal to the floor, powering the Mustang forward into the intersection, then turning left at the last second.

As if in slow motion, the rear end of my car gets loose causing it to careen toward the wall of the freeway underpass. I try to correct my mistake by counter-steering, but it's no use. I feel the rear passenger side wheel clip the curb just before the rear quarter panel smashes into the freeway support pillar. A punch to the face sends my head shooting backwards into the seat.

Lifting my head slightly, I try to look around, but the pain in my face has blurred my vision. Every last breath has been squeezed out of my lungs, and I gasp for air. A burning sensation blossoms across my neck and chest as my vision quickly fades.

Shouting snaps me back to reality as strong hands reach over and loosen my seat belt. I'm pulled out of the car and placed gently on the ground. I watch as a strange man removes his coat, folding it into a square and placing it beneath my aching head. People are talking to me, but I can't understand what they are saying.

Chapter 6

Keegan

DAMMIT! I CHOOSE TO STOP AND CHECK on Lucy instead of following her tail. The rear quarter panel took the brunt of the crash, but she is going to be nervous and quite possibly injured. I try not to consider what could have happened if I wasn't following Lucy home. Her presence on my therapy couch earlier did not help me get a handle on her mentality or confidence level, so I decided to follow and observe her.

I have called my contact at the local PD and alerted him to the need for a quick clean-up of the accident. Lucy cannot know that I'm following her, so I decide to do the Good Samaritan thing and see what happens.

Opening the door to her Mustang, it's apparent she took a hard blow to the face and chest from the airbag.

That'll leave a mark. I speak to her soothingly, but she doesn't stir. Raising my voice, I continue talking to her and gently grab her arm.

Lucy begins to move and opens her eyes. Those same pools of chocolate I saw earlier are staring back at me.

"Hey, are you ok? Does anything hurt?"

Her head falls back against the seat again, but I know she is awake, as I can see her rubbing her thumb against her thigh – her skirt riding up dangerously close to her crotch.

Stop staring at her crotch! Game on, dude. Unbuckling her belt, I lift her tenderly from the seat, managing to get her out of the car and onto the ground without further jarring her body. Shedding my jacket, I place it under her head hoping to ease the hardness of the concrete.

"Hey- so I called the police. They should be here in a moment. What happened?" I say.

Lifting her upper body, she attempts to sit up. I grab her arm to steady her.

"You should lie down. What if you have internal injuries and don't know it? Please." The sound of police units and ambulance sirens disturbs the quiet of the evening. The exhaust of the few cars driving by makes me nauseous.

"I'm Keegan. What's your name?"

"Lucy," she says quietly.

"Can I call somebody for you? I think you will need to go to the hospital and get checked out by a doctor."

The fear in her eyes is apparent.

"I don't have anyone to call. My purse, my phone…can you grab them out of my car?"

Hesitant to leave her side, I do as she asks. Lowering

myself into the car, I squeeze into the driver seat and look around for a purse or phone. I find them on the passenger-side floor, but I'm able to grab her things without having to contort my body into a pretzel. I hear the paramedics talking to Lucy behind me. Exiting the Mustang, I stand to the side while Lucy's injuries are assessed.

Walking out of earshot, I grab my vibrating phone from my pocket and answer.

"Hello?"

"Keegan, what the hell are you doing? This is a blind operation, and you are in the middle of a giant shit storm now."

"I know, Boss, but I couldn't risk leaving her. She was being tailed, and I'm concerned for her safety."

"Yeah, I get it. Make up some story and get out of there. Maybe she will forget your face if you leave quickly enough."

"Ok, Boss." Hanging up, I slip the phone into my pocket and walk back to Lucy. My buddy with the local police department has shown up but doesn't reveal my identity.

"You a witness?" he asks me.

"Not really. Only saw the car bounce off the wall." He pretends to jot down a few notes and my contact information, then tells me I can leave. Lucy is being readied for transport via stretcher, so I walk to her side and try to hand her the belongings I retrieved from her car. She grabs my arm in a panic.

"Please stay," she cries, her eyes begging me.

"I really shouldn't. Look, here is your stuff, lady. Hope you aren't too banged up." I begin my retreat when Lucy's pleading voice rips open my heart.

"I don't have anyone. Can you please meet me at the hospital?"

Without slowing my step I respond, "Sorry, that's not really my thing. Good luck." Jogging to my truck, I hop in and leave the scene. The tunes from my iPod blast into my brain as I drive away. I'm such a dick. What asshole would abandon a scared, injured woman to fend for herself?

Keeping my shit together is going to be tough. Something about Lucy makes me want to protect her, and it has nothing to do with her case. Fuck it – I have a job to do. I wasn't supposed to meet her this way, and now the operation will have to be altered. I hit the gas hoping the sooner I get home, the less likely I will do something stupid.

I walk through the sliding doors of the emergency room and quietly speak to the admitting receptionist.

What the fuck am I doing? Murphy is going to kick my ass when he finds out I disobeyed his orders to leave the scene.

Walking down the hall, I peer into the rooms looking for her. I find her at the end of the cluster of rooms, alone.

"Hey. How are you feeling?"

She opens her big brown eyes and stares at me. Her eyes portray no emotion.

"I'm fine. Just waiting to get out of here. No concussion or broken bones," she says, then turns her eyes away from my gaze.

"Can I call someone to give you a ride home? Family or friends?"

"The battery in my phone died, so I don't have anyone's number, and I don't have any family that can come get me," she says, defeated.

"May I give you a ride home? It's the least I can do for being a douche bag and leaving you by yourself back there."

"I don't take rides from strangers," the tone of her voice flat.

"Fair enough. Would you like to see my driver's license? It even has my correct home address listed." Her eyebrow lifts slightly at my question. Uncomfortable seconds pass before she finally answers.

"Ok. Let me see it."

Reaching into my back pocket for my wallet, I remove my driver's license and hold it up for her, careful to keep my thumb over that small symbol that denotes that I'm a member of law enforcement. Her hand reaches for the license, but I move it away from her grasp.

"I need to hold it, or you can leave," she says impatiently.

Glad that she isn't gullible, I hand over my card, and she inspects it thoroughly.

"What is this little symbol in the corner? My license doesn't have that. Is this fake?"

I give her my standard response when people ask about my work. "I don't like to discuss work in my private life, but I am in law enforcement."

Her eyes look me over as if she's trying to find something on my body that will confirm my statement. I notice when her eyes linger near my crotch and realize I'm sporting a decent bulge. She catches me watching her and turns away, blushing. The slight pink of her cheeks makes her look so innocent.

"I would appreciate a ride home, thanks. Can you wait outside until I'm done, please?"

"Yeah, sure. I can do that." Leaving the room, I adjust my cock so my wood isn't as obvious. What the hell is wrong with me? Getting hard for some stranger in a hospital bed? I need to get laid. I take a seat in the corner of the waiting area away from the blaring television, using the quiet to mentally plan how to proceed in handling this situation. Half an hour later, the nurse wheels Lucy out into the waiting room.

"All set?"

"Sure," she responds, despondent.

"My car is just outside," I say to the nurse who nods and follows me.

I open the door to my truck as the nurse wheels Lucy closer. She stands on shaky legs but waves off the hand I offer to her. She slowly, but easily, climbs in and thanks the nurse for her help. I walk around the back of my truck, hoping this drive goes smoothly. I climb in and crank the engine. The deep roar of the after-market exhaust system disrupts the quiet of the evening.

"Nice truck, Keegan," Lucy says, without looking at me.

"It's not bad," I say. I pull up the GPS on my dash monitor and ask Lucy for her address, even though I already know where she lives. I set the location, then steer my truck away from the hospital.

"Hey, I'm glad that you aren't hurt. What happened to

cause you to crash? I didn't see any other cars."

"I would rather not talk about it right now. I'm tired, and angry that my car is destroyed. I waited months to find the perfect one, and now it will never be the same. I know it's stupid to worry about a car, but it's like my baby," defeat apparent in her voice.

"I get it. Are you from SoCal? Because I was born and raised here in the car culture."

"Same here. My car has got to look good, have at least eight cylinders, and enough torque to plant your body into the seat." I see the corner of her mouth turn up into a smile.

We approach Lucy's neighborhood, and I ask if her roommates can give her a ride to work tomorrow. I know she lives alone, but I need to give the appearance of not knowing anything about her life, as if I was truly a stranger.

"I don't have roommates. It's just me and my tiny little house, but I'll be fine. This is it. Just up here on the left. The white house with the white fence in front." I stop in front of the modest bungalow-style home, put my truck in park, and open my door. But before I can climb down, Lucy stops me.

"No need to walk me up to the door. I'll be fine. But thank you for the consideration and the ride home. I'm grateful," she says.

"Well, if you're sure. Hope you aren't too banged up tomorrow. Take care of yourself, Lucy."

"Thanks." She smiles briefly, and closes the door on our conversation. I watch her until the front door closes and a light inside illuminates the window. I drive away, considering where this case is going to lead and just how safe is Lucy living alone?

Chapter 7

Lucy

I LOCK THE DEADBOLT BEHIND ME AND DROP my purse on the table next to the door. What the hell is going on with my life? My car is damaged, I met some strange man in a sex club, and then I let a perfect stranger drive me home. A stranger whose home address I memorized along with his curious hazel eyes.

Anxiety is engulfing me. Did I take my medication yesterday or today? I feel out of control, and that is not a comforting feeling. I turn the handles on the bathtub to get the water flowing.

Pulling out a bottle of my favorite white wine, I uncork it and give myself a nice pour. Quietly walking back into the bathroom, I disrobe and slide gently into the tub. The warmth of the water caressing my skin helps ease my rapidly beating heart. I reach over into the tiered stand next to the tub to retrieve a candle and the book of matches I keep hidden behind the assortment of bath bombs, scrubs, and lotions. I allow the comforting scent of vanilla to invade my senses.

It's just life, I tell myself. It was just a car accident. That stranger at the sex club is recommended by Andrea, and she would never put me in harm's way. Relax! You're just a spaz, I tell myself. The cool, fruity liquid slides down my throat, as I mentally try to talk myself off the ledge I have climbed.

After polishing off my glass of wine, I pull the plug on the bathtub and get out, in search of another pair of my favorite pajamas. I walk into the living area of my tiny bungalow, sit down at my desk, and power up the computer.

Focus, Lucy, focus! I need to prepare for my presentation tomorrow because I need this deal. I need the commission to pay my bills so I can keep my house and to fix my car so I can get to work. What If I lose this deal? My mind is overcome with the what-ifs that are constantly nagging me to work harder.

My greatest fear is not having a place to live. How does one even live in a car? How does one get a job without having a home address? This scenario has run through my mind for the preceding three or four years. I know it's irrational to consider, but my fear of being homeless never seems to ease. Something else I need to discuss with Andrea. Dammit! Focus, focus, focus.

Keegan

Driving away from Lucy's house, fear creeps into my gut as I consider the events of the evening. I stop at a convenience store a few blocks away to load up on snacks, energy drinks, and bottled water. Then I jump back into my truck and make my way back toward Lucy's neighborhood. I find a discreet place to park a few houses north of her bungalow. Fortunately, there are no overnight parking restrictions, so I'm safe here for a few hours.

Watching the shadows around and inside her house, I wonder just what it is that makes Lucy tick. I read her case file and consider the incident that changed the trajectory of her life so drastically. The only thing missing from her file are her psychological records. Notes in the file state that Lucy's psychologist refused to turn over her records without a lawful subpoena and declined to make a statement about her care and mental health.

Raising the binoculars, I observe the area surrounding Lucy's house, trying to get a feel for her neighbors and all the normal neighborhood activity, so I will know when something is amiss.

The sun's rays begin to rise over the mountains to the east. Embarrassed that I nodded off while surveilling a location, I lift the binoculars to my sleepy eyes and study the small bungalow and the quiet neighborhood surrounding it.

Two hours have passed, and there is no movement in

Lucy's home. I would think she needs to get to work as it is approaching 9 a.m. I can't risk being seen, and I can't knock on her door to check on her. So I stay put, scooting deeper into my seat, hoping to avoid detection by a neighbor.

At 9:30, Lucy comes tearing out of her house looking disheveled in a black skirt suit and heels, dragging a large bag along with her. It appears to be some type of computer bag, but it's big enough to hold a week's worth of my clothes.

She paces the sidewalk for several minutes until a car pulls up and stops in front of her. As soon as she hops into the back seat, the car speeds away. Slowly falling into traffic behind Lucy's hired car, it appears we are headed to downtown Los Angeles.

This time of morning the traffic has subsided, allowing us to travel at a slow but steady pace. Weaving through the back streets of the valley, we merge onto the oldest freeway in Los Angeles, the 110 or Pasadena freeway. There is a maximum speed limit of 55 miles per hour on this highway, but we are doing a staggering 70 mph as we approach downtown.

Lucy's car exits into Koreatown, and I realize we are nowhere near her office. The car stops abruptly outside a high rise. Lucy jumps out and runs into the building with her big bag in tow. Realizing she may be here for a bit, I get back onto the freeway to return to Lucy's house so that I can place surveillance equipment in and around her home to assure we adequately watch over her. Checking my watch, I make the return drive in just under twenty minutes.

Before I exit my vehicle, I change into a nondescript shirt I have with the spare clothes I keep under the backseat of my truck. Then I carefully slip into Lucy's backyard, making sure I am not seen by her neighbors. The privacy of her yard makes it easy for me to pick my way into her house. After placing several listening devices and one small camera around the home, I take a minute and look through a few drawers in her house, hoping to get an inside piece of information about Lucy's life.

Finding nothing but takeout menus, bills, and notepads, I exit through the back door, lock up behind me, and walk confidently around the side of the house to her front door, where I leave a note wedged between the door and the framing.

Hey Lucy,

Dropped by to see how you are feeling.

Keegan

Walking quickly back to my truck, I get in and drive away, hoping my plan comes together.

Lucy

How could I forget my alarm on such an important day? I'm late, and Beau isn't responding to my texts – so typical when I need him. But he is probably still meeting with the client. God, I hope he is still with the client. I pop gumballs into my mouth, hoping the burst of sugar will keep me on my toes for the meeting. I usually have a small stash of them in my purse for such emergencies. A mini volcano of chewed gum is now hidden in a plastic baggie at the bottom of my purse.

After what seems like forever, my taxi pulls up to the client's office building. I hit the sidewalk in a half jog, half walk. The last thing I want to do is trip on my way in, because that is something that would totally happen to me. Rushing to the elevator, I continuously hit the button for the 9th floor until the doors finally close.

My foot taps furiously on the floor and my hands wring themselves to calloused while I wait for the elevator to reach its destination. I fluff my hair one last time as the elevator doors open. There in the hallway are Beau and the client happily chatting and shaking hands. Just as I step out of the elevator, Beau comes rushing forward and forces me back in, while saying a quick thank you and goodbye to our client.

The doors close, and I'm left staring at Beau, waiting for him to say something. I fucked up this account. I know it was me. I should have been here to answer any financial questions or to thoroughly explain the bond terms. Beau still has not looked my way.

The soft elevator music has done nothing to cool my emotions. I'm screwed! I stare at the ground contemplating how I can explain my absence without seeming incompetent.

"We got the deal," Beau says confidently. I lift my eyes to meet his gaze and see the hint of a smirk on his face.

"Thank God. I'm so sorry, Beau. I was in a car accident last night, and somehow I missed my alarm this morning. Then I had to wait for a taxi to show up because I don't have a car. Thank you for covering for me."

"I didn't cover for you. I made the deal myself, as it seemed the only way to salvage the client," he says boldly. Shocked at what I'm hearing, I'm rendered speechless.

"But I did all the important work. I found the financing. I compiled all the research and evaluated the ratios. I did everything necessary to sell this deal!" I say in my loudest inside-voice.

"But you did not sell the product to the client. You were not at the meeting. I'm sorry, Lucy. I had no choice."

I'm so fucked! I need this deal so my sales numbers remain positive. The same fears that grip my life on a weekly basis return. How will I pay my bills? My mortgage is due next week. If I lose my job, this will be a huge black mark on my resumé, and nobody will even think of hiring me. I have no car at the moment. How am I going to get to interviews?

"Why are you acting like this?" I say with despair. "I need this job, this sale." My voice rises, drawing a few looks from the other people in the lobby.

"Lucy, you need to settle down," Beau says weakly. I want to scream at him, blame this on him. And doesn't he know the general rule of the universe, when you tell a woman to settle down it only inflames them more? We exit the office building, and I stop in the courtyard, realizing I don't have a ride.

"Can I grab a ride back to the office with you? My car is not available at the moment," I say, as though what just occurred is water under the bridge.

"Of course. What are you going to tell the bosses?" he asks as we hop in his Passat and begin the drive back to the office.

"The truth, I guess. I made a mistake, and it won't happen again."

"Yeah, the truth in this case is probably the best way to go," he agrees. I want to strangle Beau right now. On the outside I appear relaxed, but on the inside my blood is boiling.

We arrive back at the First SoCal building and ride the elevator up to our floor together. But as soon as we exit the elevator, we go our separate ways without another word. I can't help but think I was completely betrayed by Beau. He could have easily sold this deal to the client on both our behalves, despite my absence. I did all the work necessary to pitch the client. He merely took my analysis and the marketing notes included in my report and presented them to the client. I'm not even sure if what he presented was correct. Oh, fuck! What if he misrepresented parts of the deal, and the client didn't catch it before the agreement was affirmed? Oh, no! My mind goes into overdrive considering every worst-case scenario imaginable.

I drop my bag behind my desk and am startled when Mr. Lewis's secretary, Elaine, walks in behind me.

"Lucy, Mr. Lewis would like to see you in his office."

"Yes, thank you, Elaine." I follow Elaine to the opposite corner of our floor. You can do this, Lucy. You can do this, I tell myself over and over and over.

"Go right in, Lucy," Elaine says as she takes her position at the desk outside Mr. Lewis's office.

Straightening my skirt, I try to walk confidently into the office, but fear has accumulated in my throat. My voice squeaks as I alert my boss to my presence. "Hello, Mr.

Lewis. You wanted to see me?" I feel like a puppy cowering in a corner.

"Yes, Lucy, please have a seat." He smiles warmly. I often think Mr. Lewis would be the kind of father I would choose, if given the opportunity. He has always been supportive and understanding and one of my biggest cheerleaders. But he is also results-driven, and I fear this may be the final straw that breaks his support of me.

His kind, brown eyes betray no emotion. A genuine smile extends across his face. He follows that smile with a loud sigh and the removal of his reading glasses. He rubs his forehead gently, as if wiping away the thought of an annoying conversation.

"Lucy, what is going on with you? You jeopardized an important account this morning by not showing up for your meeting. From what I understand, important questions were asked that required your expertise, and you were not available to answer them," he says in his most sympathetic manner.

"I know, Mr. Lewis. I could not be more embarrassed, and I really have no excuse, but I was in a car accident last night. While I'm not physically injured, just a little sore from bumps and bruises, apparently the rush of adrenaline and subsequent shock of the incident left me a bit confused, and I failed to set my alarm clock. I woke up this morning sitting at my computer, hunched over the desk. I should have taken measures to guarantee my timely appearance this morning," I say honestly.

"Well, I'm sorry to hear about your accident, and I'm glad to know you are uninjured for the most part. In the future, I would suggest you alert a co-worker should you have something happen that could jeopardize your work here. I know you are a hard worker, Lucy. Let's take this as a learning experience and move forward."

"Thank you, Mr. Lewis. I won't disappoint you again."

"Now get to work on mining some new clients."

"Yes, sir," I say, as I stand and make a hasty retreat back to my desk. I'm grateful that the boss seems to understand what happened, but I'm left wholly irritated with Beau. We are friends – I would have covered for him if the situation were reversed. What is his deal?

Plopping into my chair, I reach down and open the drawer that houses my precious gumballs. A sound that could only be described as white noise fills my mind. Goosebumps appear on my arms and legs, the hair on my arms standing at attention. The movements of the office become amplified, as if in slow motion. I watch my hand shake, unable to control its movement. Somebody is fucking with me. But why? Why the hell is this happening to me? There in the drawer, next to a bag of gumballs, is a bottle of EnsureLife—you know, that fortified drink they give to old people or others who are nutritionally deficient? That is the EnsureLife lying in my drawer. The only people on Earth who could know its significance are the people who kidnapped me, the FBI, or my therapists and doctors.

This has to be a joke. I look around for cameras or something that would make this all seem like a colossal prank, but there is nobody else anywhere near my desk. The vein in my throat pulses in time with the beat of my heart. I send a quick note to my bosses and let them know I am taking a few hours of personal time. Slamming the drawer shut and grabbing my bag, I make a beeline for the stairs.

The taxi I called to my office drops me at the car rental, where I pick up an unexciting, but functional, compact car. As the engine clicks to life, I feel none of the relief I find while driving my Mustang. I drive toward one of my few places of comfort, Andrea's office.

Fortunately, Andrea has a cancellation, and I only have to wait an hour to see her. By the time she calls me into her office, I am an anxious, freaked-out mess.

After talking through what has happened over the last few days, we decide I need to contact somebody in law enforcement to discuss the possible reappearance of my kidnappers, and I need to figure out what is up with Beau. Andrea is extremely concerned about the situation and wants me to contact my employer as well. We argue about this, because I'm afraid of the consequences that may occur if I reveal my entire kidnapping and reappearance. I'm anxious, and I'm scared, but I also don't want to overreact. I'm afraid of becoming that crazy girl who thinks food appearing in her desk is ominous. It's the stigma of mental illness that I fear. The looks from family and friends and the whispering behind my back about how I used to be normal. It has taken years to leave those fears behind, and I'm going to be 100% positive about my current predicament before I bring my employer and family into the fray.

The hour of talking with Andrea has left me drained, so I decide to wait until tomorrow to contact the FBI about my situation. Tonight, I want a nice long bath and my bed.

Chapter 8

Keegan

I'M SITTING IN A RAMEN SHOP NOT FAR FROM my house that I know is Lucy's go-to dinner after her therapy sessions. Lucy is a creature of habit—a predictable, easy target—which is why I need to befriend her—to get closer to her, so I can keep her safe while we work the case. Lucy walks into the shop right on time and takes her place in the order line. She places her order then proceeds to the take-out counter to wait for her number to be called.

I look at my phone pretending to read *The Daily Mail*. It has the strangest mix of stories, but I know it won't distract me from my surroundings.

I look up at Lucy hoping she raises her head enough to look around the small eatery. Unfortunately, she keeps her head down as though she is reading something on her phone.

Lucy's order number is called. She grabs her bag of food and walks toward the exit. This is my chance.

"Hey, Lucy. How are you doing?" She startles and looks at me like I'm a three-headed toad. A moment passes, then a small smile graces her face. She raises her hand in a small wave and takes a few steps toward my table.

There are twelve tables in this small eatery, so it doesn't appear strange that I noticed her walking through the restaurant. The last thing I want to do is spook her.

"Keegan, hi. What are you doing here? I mean, hi, I'm fine, how are you?"

I smile eagerly. "I'm doing well. Just getting a bite to eat. Hey, would you like to join me? I'm still getting settled in town and don't know many people. I would appreciate the company."

Lucy looks hesitant, and I know she is going to decline.

"I really just want to get home. It's been a long day. But thanks for the offer."

"Please? I'm just glad to see someone I know." That sounds so desperate, I think.

"I really shouldn't," Lucy responds.

"Yes, you really should. Here have a seat." I reach for her food bag and encourage her to sit across from me in the small booth.

"Well, I guess I can stay for a bit. This place has the best ramen in the valley."

"It's my first time here, but I have to agree, the food is amazing! So, how are you feeling?"

"I'm a little bit sore from the accident but only minor aches and pains. Thank you again for helping me last night."

She keeps her eyes focused on preparing her food, first placing her chicken in the steaming broth, followed by bean sprouts and some other weed like vegetable. Lastly, she scoops a small dollop of chili paste into her soup and stirs.

"I'm glad you are all right. What is the story with your car? How bad is the damage?"

"Ugh, don't ask. The rear axle is bent, and there is some body damage. It needs a new wheel, brakes, and air bag. Hopefully, it will be fixed in a few weeks. I have this horrible little compact sedan as a rental now, and the sooner I can get rid of it, the better. I've never owned a car with a 4-cylinder engine." She smiles and glances up at me briefly. When her eyes reach mine, she looks away and her cheeks blush slightly.

"4 cylinders is no bueno. I agree with you on that."

"What brings you to this part of town? I saw your address on your license. You live east of here, so this isn't in your neighborhood."

"I drive through here on my way home from work. There isn't much to eat around my house, so I have been trying little places here and there. It's funny, I've been away for ten years working on the east coast, and so much has changed that I almost don't feel like this is my home anymore. Almost, but not quite, if you know what I mean."

"I get it. I've never left the valley, so I guess the changes have grown on me. Except the traffic. Man, the traffic gets worse every year. There is almost no rush hour because all day is rush hour. So what took you away to the east coast?"

she asks with genuine interest.

"A job. An adventure, I guess," I say quickly, hoping we can move away from the subject. "Why isn't a nice girl like you eating dinner with her boyfriend or getting ready to go out tonight?" I say, waiting for her eyes to meet mine.

"No boyfriend for me. Going out isn't really my thing," she says quietly, our eyes meeting briefly.

"What about you? No girlfriend followed you back here to California?"

"Nope. Been single for a while, and I keep busy, so I haven't really felt like I needed a girlfriend." I look her in the eyes, and for the first time since I met her, she doesn't look away. I feel a flutter in my chest and the hair on the back of my neck stands at attention. I don't want to lead her on, so I do the only thing a dick like me can do. I say, "I have plenty of girls sniffing around. I don't need any of them in my way. I have fun. No promises." I fake a confident smirk.

"I get it, really I do. My friend, Beau, is the same way. Always a different girl, no promises, no broken hearts, no needy girls hanging all over him." A hint of disappointment flashes in her eyes. "Well, Keegan, I'm going to get out of here. Thanks for the company." She gathers her litter and piles it quickly into her to-go bag. I stand and grab her bag, taking a step closer to her, blocking her from leaving.

"Thanks for having dinner with me, Lucy. I'm glad you are doing well. Maybe we can do this again sometime," I say hopefully.

"I enjoyed it, Keegan." Walking away, she turns her head back to me, a faint smile on her face and says, "I'll see you around." And then she's gone.

I sit down and let out a deep breath. I think it went ok, but I'm still confused about Lucy. She is twenty-five years old and seems to lead a quiet life, just going to work and back home. Her case file says much of the same. Why is such a pretty girl hiding from life? I know what happened to her. The kidnapping had to have been difficult, and I recall something about a hospitalization in her file as well. Does she really not see her life passing by her? Her shy demeanor seems like an act, but maybe it isn't.

I toss our trash in the bin and decide to hit the gym with more questions in my mind than when I first sat down with Lucy. Hopefully, lifting some heavy weights will clear my mind.

Lucy

Home, safe and sound. To my dismay, I feel grateful to have run into Keegan and to have sat with him through dinner. He doesn't know me from before, and I didn't feel like he was staring at me with *that look*. That look that I get from old friends and family who survey me with pity because I'm so far gone – so broken from my former self. And I can't blame them one bit. I am broken. I'm so fucked up in the head, I wonder if this is truly who I am at all.

My therapy with Andrea has helped me move on from the incident, but I still haven't forgiven myself for what has happened to me since. I can't forgive myself for being broken, for being afraid, for letting my body go, for every single regret that I have.

When I was in high school, I was at a party drinking and having a good time with a friend. Nothing unusual for me. I was outgoing and fearless. I had lots of friends but I wasn't the most popular or the prettiest girl at school. I was happy being me.

That evening, my drink was spiked, and I was removed from the party, unbeknownst to my friends. I woke up in a house with dirty white walls, shackled to the floor by a long nylon rope. There was nothing in the room but an old trundle bed, minus the trundle, and one blanket and pillow. To my horror, I was wearing only my bra and underwear.

I remember crying for what seemed like hours. At some point, a man came into the room and deposited a container of prepared Mac Made Easy – that no-brainer kind of mac and cheese that smells awful—along with a bottle of EnsureLife to wash down the food.

Promptly leaving and closing the door behind him, this was the extent of my interaction with the kidnappers for more than two weeks.

When I think about that time in my life, I grow restless and angry, so I try and distract myself. I grab my iPod and headphones and hit the streets.

I don't live in the nicest neighborhood, but it is safe, with wide sidewalks and large, mature trees. The cool October night is a welcome change from the warm Santa Ana winds that have been heating up the valley over the last month.

I hit the pop music playlist on my iPod to keep my mind from wandering back to the incident. I enjoy the crunch of fall leaves under my feet and the darkness of the sky overhead. It's during these walks that I feel safe, invisible, free. Free because I don't feel the sympathetic stares of people from my past or the judging looks from anyone in my life. You know, those looks that say, "She would be so pretty if she lost some weight." And even worse are the looks that never even materialize – when others disregard you as a whole because you don't meet their physical expectations. I can't help that this bothers me. It is something I live with every day, and every morning I wake up hoping I won't see that look in someone's eyes – the look of pity. Tears threaten to stain my cheeks, but I battle them. Not tonight tears – you aren't going to win tonight. I hit the mind-numbing playlist on my iPod, and my thoughts are disintegrated by the heavy pace of vintage Metallica. I can always count on *One* or *Ride the Lightening* to stop my mind from wandering.

The playlist runs out as I slowly creep up the front porch of my home. Inside, I toe off my shoes and walk into the kitchen to get a glass of water. Grabbing my phone, I notice a few recent text messages. Beau. What does he want?

7:11 p.m.
Beau: *Where R U?*
Beau: *on ur porch*
Beau: *what is going on*
Beau: *r u ok? U r always home*
8:02 p.m.
Me: *was walking*
Me: *what did u need?*

Beau: *came by 2 hang out*

Me: *why*

Beau: *wanted to binge Game of Thrones*

Me: *not tonight*

Beau: *good cuz I'm with someone and about to go to pound town*

Beau: *out*

Does Beau really think we are good after what he did to me? Men. They really are fucking clueless.

Beau and I have been friends since he started at First SoCal about a year after me. We were easy friends, never asking too much of each other, never confiding too heavily or needing one another. I have come to rely on the stability of our friendship, but I'm starting to wonder if that was all a façade. Maybe I'm just blind to see that Beau is not the friend I had thought he was.

Enough thinking, Lucy! Dammit! Get out your vibrator or a glass of wine or something to stop you from thinking. I startle at the ding of an incoming text:

Master: *Tomorrow, 6 p.m.*

Me: *Yes, sir*

Master: *Go to our room, get comfortable on the chaise, and keep your eyes on my painting. No questions.*

With that, I grab a bottle of wine from the fridge and fill my glass close to full. I plug my phone into the charger, set my alarm, and turn the volume all the way to max. I get comfortable on the sofa and turn on my favorite crime show, *Dateline*. I have seen every episode, but I enjoy the mystery, the motive of murder. And it always seems to put me to sleep.

Chapter 9

Keegan

AFTER OUR END-OF-THE-WEEK CASE update, I walk upstairs to the department library and check out Lucy's entire case file. When initially read into her case, I was given a brief synopsis of her kidnapping and subsequent history. Something broke Lucy, and I want to understand what happened to her.

I open the thick file and begin reading. The kidnapping was fairly simple. She was drugged and carried away from a party by a kid named Grayson. Apparently, he was the son of the mastermind—a man who sought revenge against Lucy's father for a failed business venture.

Mr. John Meadows, Lucy's father, is a successful insurance broker who owns an agency that employs about one hundred people and generates millions of dollars in revenue each year. Generally speaking, Meadows Insurance has happy clients and content employees.

During the trial of Lucy's kidnappers, corruption was claimed by the defendants against Meadows Insurance, but no hard evidence was presented. Defense claims stated that John Meadows, as their business insurance broker, drastically under-insured the business and its equipment. Documents submitted into evidence showed extremely high premiums but with appropriate policy limits. The issued policy from the insurance carrier showed the same premium but a fraction of the coverage for the business. Because the trial was about Lucy's kidnapping, John Meadows' impropriety was deemed not relevant to the defense and removed from consideration.

The plan involved kidnapping Lucy for a ransom which would restore the family business that was destroyed in a warehouse fire. The business was drastically underinsured as previously stated, and the insurance payout covered only the cleanup of the site. Meadows Insurance had all the papers to back up their work, including the signature of the defendant acknowledging their coverage agreement. Having no viable defense in regards to Lucy's kidnapping, the defendants, Kyle and Jennifer Smith, were found guilty and handed twelve and fifteen year sentences in federal prison. Their son, Grayson, who was the lure that drugged Lucy, was sentenced as an adult to 10 years prison, followed by 5 years of probation.

Lucy's appearance at the trial was brief. She testified against Grayson and explained how she came to meet him at the party the night of her disappearance. When it came time to pinpoint her captors, Lucy could not identify them because they had worn masks every time they entered her room. While in captivity, Lucy was not treated poorly, raped, or abused. But she was found chained to the floor, wearing nothing but her underwear, in a room equipped with a rickety bed and a tiny bathroom.

The FBI took almost three weeks to track down Lucy's location and her kidnappers. She was rescued from her captors in a daring, early morning raid on the home in an unincorporated part of Los Angeles near Van Nuys. Crucial testimony came from the FBI agents and Kidnap and Ransom team retained by Mr. Meadow's insurance company who identified the defendants as the occupants of the home where Lucy was rescued. There was no question that the minor son had drugged Lucy and removed her from the party, per his statement to authorities.

In the aftermath of Lucy's rescue, she did not return for the last few months of high school and was instead given home study. She declined to walk with the rest of her class at graduation. Lucy retreated from life, did not see her friends, and eventually, her mother moved them south into Orange County. The psychological reports in the file note Lucy's fall into a deep depression in the year following her rescue. Weekly counseling sessions were attended, but her depression continued and eventually worsened to the point that Lucy's mother had her enter an inpatient program for thirty days of intense therapy.

At the same time, Lucy's relationship with her father soured. While they were on speaking terms, John Meadows appeared too busy with his personal life to bother with

Lucy's recovery, getting remarried and opening a second branch of his insurance agency. The file denotes Mr. Meadows' fondness for the latest Mercedes, the newest watch, and top shelf liquor. I guess Lucy's dad was too busy living the good life to pay any attention to his suffering daughter.

Lucy attended college during this time, opting to do most of her course work online. Her attendance at traditional classes was spotty, but she passed all of her courses with little trouble.

The file contains very little about her personal life in the subsequent years. Because there appeared to no longer be a threat to her life, the FBI ceased monitoring Lucy and documenting her activities once the trial recessed.

Flipping back to the front of the file, I glance through the recent case notes concerning the reopening of the investigation. Apparently, there has been jailhouse chatter regarding revenge against the Meadows family. Lucy, being an easy target, has been mentioned in the chatter frequently. Normally, simple jailhouse gossip would not warrant opening an investigation, but a life insurance policy for Lucy was found, purchased by an offshore company based in Belize. With no way to track the owners of the life insurance policy due to strict financial laws, the FBI deemed the information curious. In addition, investigators could not uncover any links between Lucy and the offshore company.

The life insurance policy was enough proof for the FBI to consider the matter an open case. So here I am, tasked with following Lucy and searching for leads close to her while my colleagues investigate everything else.

Lucy has few people in her life, all of whom check out with clean records, no large debts, and no suspicious hobbies or expenses. Unfortunately, I'm going to have to get more information from the girl herself. And she is not going to like it.

Lucy

I plow through my work day, manage to book a few new client meetings, and have lunch with my work friend, Kristy. She is my other close friend at the office, but I know better than to confide anything important to her. She is recognized as the office gossip. If there is something to be known, Kristy is the Nosy Nellie who will uncover everything. Regardless, we get along well. Frankly, I welcome the distraction from everything else going on in my life. The afternoon drones on, but I finish up the day strong, a few sales calls complete and my unread email left at zero. With a heavy sigh I ready myself for a long evening ahead.

I always have anxiety on therapy days. While I'm grateful for the time Andrea invests in helping me, I would be lying if I said the sessions are getting easier. Plus, today after my therapy, I have another session with The Master. I don't even know what will happen or what this will do to help me. And that gives me anxiety.

I make the drive to Griffith Park with the sunroof open, the only decent accessory on this car, enjoying the mild temperature and abundant sunshine. I park next to Andrea's house and walk up the path to the waiting area on the side of her house. It's a beautiful, peaceful space filled with lush plants and trees. I catch a glimpse of the large fountain that looms near the picture window, and there is a plush patio glider for waiting clients get comfortable. I hear the front door of Andrea's house open and close, followed by the footsteps of her previous client retreating to the street.

Several moments later, Andrea opens the French doors to her office and waves me inside. Today there is a hand-poured candle burning in the center of the table and the faint sound of jazz playing over the speakers. Andrea asks me what's been happening since I saw her yesterday.

"I ran into Keegan, that guy who helped me at the accident and hospital. He was at this ramen place near my house, and I joined him for a little while," I say while keeping my eyes on that box of rocks in front of Andrea.

"What is important about seeing him that you would tell me about it?" she asks, her hands empty, folded in her lap.

"Why no rocks today?" I say pointedly.

Andrea sighs and responds shortly, "Don't change the subject. You know I don't always use the rocks."

"Ok, I don't really know why I mentioned it. Maybe I'm a little confused at seeing him. He is a complete stranger, yet I've seen him twice this week. Is that just a coincidence? And I meet him when everything in my life is going haywire. Beau is acting oddly, I think I'm being stalked, those strange items have been planted in my desk, and now I run into some guy twice in a week?" I stare at Andrea, waiting for her to respond. She searches through the box of rocks and chooses a yellowish stone.

"What does that stone do?"

"Focus, Lucy," she says sternly and continues. "Maybe everything is a coincidence. Maybe this is all a blessing. All this turmoil in your life, as you like to call it, is causing you to really look at yourself. You appear unflustered compared to how you would have reacted in the past. I hope this means you're learning to accept some parts of yourself and have opened your mind to meeting new people. You isolate yourself and keep your few friends on very short leashes with your emotions. Are you ready to trust yourself and your emotions to more people?" she asks emphatically.

"I don't know. I feel like I want to open myself up, but can I really trust myself?"

"It's not just about trust. It's about having a little faith that you can trust people again. It's about understanding that emotions are an important part of life," Andrea says.

I have no response. Some days I just don't have the energy to talk about my feelings. Andrea knows me well, so she gives me a talk about psychological stuff. I nod and make small talk. I thank her for her time, hug her as I expect to at the end of our sessions, and walk slowly to my car. I feel mentally brain-dead, but I steer the car toward my next appointment anyway.

It's like Groundhog Day on the freeway. My head bobs forward and back with the stop-and-go traffic. My clutch foot grows tired from the constant easing in and out of the pedal. Half an hour later, I'm parked in the lot of the office building with five minutes to spare before 6 p.m.

I walk up the stairs, open the door, and turn down the

hall toward the same room I occupied yesterday. Cracking the door open, I see the lights are dim, candles are burning, and soft music is playing in the background. Dropping my bag on the floor, I remove my suit jacket and hang it on the back of the door.

Doing as instructed, I get comfortable on the lounge and close my eyes, allowing the calming music and low lights to ease the fears creeping into my brain. I try not to think of anything that will cause anxiety to flare in my gut. I mentally tap my foot in time to the music.

Suddenly, I startle and realize I had dozed off. Everything in the room appears the same, but there is an electricity in the air. I sit up so I can look behind me when he speaks.

"Eyes forward, Lucy." I do as instructed. I try to remain placid, but the butterflies thrusting in my stomach make it difficult.

"Relax and close your eyes. There is nothing to fear. We are going to start with some simple massage techniques to get you relaxed."

I feel his hand grip my ankle followed by the removal of my shoe. When both of my shoes are off, Master begins to give my feet a firm massage. He touches all those pressure points on my foot that feel as though they hold every anxiety in my body. I enjoy the skin-to-skin contact, the rhythmic pressure of his fingers, as he works to remove my pent up anxiety by way of my feet.

When it seems I couldn't relax more, Master begins massaging my legs, rubbing a light lotion across my skin, filling the air with the scent of vanilla. As his hands make their way up to the hem of my skirt, I feel the muscles in my neck tense and a fire ignites in my core.

"Calm down, Lucy. We discussed your safe word and the necessity for you to trust me," he says.

I open my eyes and look at Master, my first glimpse at the man who has commanded my trust. He looks at me intently, continuing to massage my legs as I contemplate him. A mask covers most of his face, but I can see his jaw is covered in a light stubble. His eyes are hazel, the green flecks of his irises reflecting the light. His lips are thick and heart-shaped, the bottom lip slightly fuller than the top.

He is wearing dark jeans and a white, long sleeved t-shirt pulled taught against his well-developed chest. I see the hint of a gold necklace peek out from his collar and possibly the ink of a tattoo as well, but I can't be certain in this dimly lit room. The sleeves of his shirt are pushed up close to his elbows. His forearms are corded with muscle from a healthy relationship with the heavy weight room at the gym.

"Are you done looking at me, Lucy?"

"I am," I whisper, as the heat of embarrassment washes my cheeks in a deep red. I see the slightest upturn of Master's mouth before he turns away from me. I lay there evaluating the watercolor before me once more with its subtle yet raw beauty.

"Please stand and face the painting," Master commands. I do as I am told. The warmth of his body warms my back even though we are not touching. A gradual ache blossoms in my core, my head tips back at the welcome sensation. I feel the tender pressure of his hands as he holds me by the hips.

My panties are soaked. The skin across my arms, covered in goose bumps, betrays my feelings. Master tugs me closer to him, letting my back rest against his chest, the pressure of his hands on my hips remaining gentle. The scent of him envelops me, a cross between a wooded meadow and the rich aroma of pipe tobacco.

A hand makes its way from my hip, up my arm, and rests in the center of my chest as though trying to settle my raging heart. Moments later, his touch is gone. My eyes burst open, but I learn nothing looking at the watercolor before me.

There is the click of a door closing behind me, and the lights in the room raise, signaling the end of our session.

Putting on my shoes, my mind is overcome with emotion. Overcome with want and need. The need to have human contact, to feel something, to feel anything.

I grab my purse and scurry out the door and down the stairs to my car. I throw myself into the driver seat and direct the car onto the surface street. The adrenaline coursing through my veins encourages me to drive faster, as fast as this rental car will go. I work my way through the LA traffic as quickly as possible, hoping that the safety of my home will help clear my brain. I don't like needing another person or wanting another person. If I wanted or needed someone, I would be opening myself up to heartache, because the only person I can really count on is myself. When I have allowed myself to need other people in my life, I have been met with extreme despair. I feel safer being alone, being lonely, than allowing myself to want another person in my life.

I was rescued from my kidnappers in an early morning raid of the house where I was captive. The FBI SWAT team and local police coordinated a high-powered assault on my captors, catching the entire band of kidnappers off guard, while rescuing me with no injuries. I recall sitting in the back of an ambulance for hours while police interviewed me. I was wearing nothing but my two-week worn underwear and a blanket thrown over my shoulders. Sure, I was alive and unharmed, but the year following my release really sent my brain into deep depression. When the information was revealed to me regarding the nature of my kidnapping, I became distraught. I was kidnapped for ransom as a way to get back at my father – the father who can't be bothered to have dinner with me. The father who brushed off my depression as if it were a common cold that would disappear in a few days.

The most damning part of the incident was my father's unwillingness to pay the ransom. I'm told law enforcement tried for over a week to facilitate an exchange, but my father refused. He claimed that he received expert advice not to comply with the ransom. Apparently, my father maintained a Kidnap and Ransom insurance policy on my mother and me, but the coverage was void in the United States. However, the policy issuer did agree to provide an expert advisor for this unique situation. During the trial of my kidnappers, I learned that, had my father provided the ransom, I would have been rescued about four days earlier. Sure, I wasn't harmed, but I felt thrown away, worthless – my own father wouldn't part with money to save my life. It's a hard pill to swallow when you are only eighteen years old and see your parents as your heroes. I think it was that day of the trial that my entire view of life was skewed, furthering my descent into the black hole that is depression.

But enough of remembering that crap. Snap out of it, Lucy. Fuck them, I tell myself.

I pull into my driveway, park, and walk quickly toward the back door. Before my foot hits the first of two steps, I see it. Atop my doormat is a length of nylon rope, identical to what was used to tether me to the floor during my captivity. Stumbling back to the car, fear grips my heart like a hawk to its prey. Large tear drops trickle from my eyes. I tap the number on my phone for my closest friend, Quinn, hoping she's home. The engine of the little import is angered by my desire to get away quickly. The whine of the motor as the RPMs increase does not ease my senses. Quinn picks up the call and tells me she's home – she is always home. She lives in the next city, so I merely have to navigate the traffic lights as I race to her house as fast as this cheap compact will take me.

Chapter 10

Keegan

JUST SECONDS AFTER I PARK DISCREETLY NEAR Lucy's house, she pulls out into the driveway. Thank God she has that cheap rental car with the tiny engine, or she would have beat me to her house. As quickly as she gets out of the car, she gets back in and races down the street, away from her house. Dammit. Where is she going? Making a split second decision, I decide to follow her, staying close behind. I don't worry about being seen, because I traded my truck for a forgettable car from the precinct pool of cars for use in undercover operations.

I increase the distance between our cars as she turns into another residential area. Watching Lucy stop in front of a small apartment building, she quickly jogs up to the stairway at the front of the building and disappears. Pulling my binoculars from my bag, I watch the upstairs apartments for movement. Fortunately, the curtains in the front apartment are open, and I'm able to catch a glimpse of her walking animatedly around the room.

I call Joey from my team and send him over to Lucy's house to check for a break-in or whatever may have spooked her.

Time passes and Lucy and her friend quiet down. The lights in the apartment dim, but I can still see one of them on occasion. After about an hour, a pizza deliveryman trudges up the stairway and delivers a pizza to the apartment. The curtains are still open, so I can see both women periodically walking around the room. Both appear to be talking earnestly.

Joey checks and lets me know Lucy's house is secure, but there is a stretch of rope curled up on her back porch. This seems out of place to both of us, but we are not sure what to make of it.

The lights in the apartment switch off around 11 p.m., and I assume Lucy and her friend have turned in for the evening. Joey and I agree we will tag team the surveillance on Lucy until we can determine if there is a viable threat. At 2:00 in the morning, Joey beats on my car window, startling me from a restless slumber.

"Nice work, dick," he says with a smirk on his face.

Ignoring his comment, I update him. "No movement in the apartment since 11 p.m., and no suspicious activity in the surrounding area," I tell Joey between yawns.

"The friend is Quinn Sawyer, thirty year old female. Looks as though they have been friends for more than a few years. Sawyer is quiet, has one of those online jobs where you work from home. No red flags in her background. No apparent money problems," he says.

"That's good news, man. Thanks for the info. I'll check back in a few hours," I tell Joey. I watch as he walks back to his vehicle and opens and closes the door with little noise. I start the engine to my surveillance car and turn it toward my home to catch a few hours of sleep.

Lucy

After a restless night's sleep, I convince Quinn to drive back to my house with me to see if everything is okay to return. What two scared women are going to do when faced with an intruder or kidnapper is beyond my mental grasp at the moment, but we decide to drive by and check things out, then go from there. We shower and dress for the day and proceed toward my home.

The events of the last few days have left me physically and emotionally drained. I feel like I'm running on fumes, so I hit the drive-thru for a venti iced mocha – my go-to drink when I'm dragging ass. Quinn orders a green tea. I don't know how she drinks that stuff. It tastes like nothing. I'm just glad I convinced her to leave the apartment. She is a bit of a hermit and doesn't like to go out in public much. But her concern for my safety outweighed her need to be at home.

We enter my house through the front door, armed with

our large purses and cups of caffeine. After walking through my tiny house and determining all the doors and windows are secure and nothing else is out of place, I walk into the bedroom for a fresh change of clothes. I check my reflection in the bathroom mirror, and when I'm prepared for work, I walk into the living room to check on Quinn.

She is one of my only friends who knows the entire story of my kidnapping. I don't know what she did with the rope on my back porch, but I know it's gone. We exit through the backyard to double-check the area for any suspicious objects and that nothing is out of place.

"Maybe you should stay at my house until this mess blows over," Quinn says as we drive back to her apartment.

"I'll think about it. But we both like our space, and I don't know if all this stuff showing up in odd places is really anything at all. I called the Bureau and alerted them to all of the things that have been happening lately, and they said they would check into it. I don't know what that means, but I feel like I have people on my side," I say solemnly.

"Ok, Lulu, but call me if you get scared. Or better yet, just come over anytime," she tells me.

"You know I hate when you call me Lulu," I say with laughter in my voice. "But thanks, Quinney. I owe you."

"And you know that I hate Quinney more than anything, bitch," she says as we pull up to her apartment. We are both giggling like twelve year olds.

"Thanks, Q. For everything," I say as she climbs from my car. Before closing the door, she turns to me with another smile.

"I'm always here for you, Lucy. Please be aware of your

surroundings. Text me later."

And she is off, walking leisurely to the stairwell of her apartment building. I wait until I see her wave at me from the front window. I drive away laughing, while Quinn is doing some freak dance in the window for all the neighbors to see.

I'm pulled away from my laughing fit when my phone dings signaling an incoming text. Seeing Beau's name in the notifications, I decide to pull over and handle this problem.

Beau: *Pitch meeting @ 10:30?*

Me: *Just me today*

Beau: *What?*

Me: *I'm handling*

It's no surprise my phone is now ringing with an incoming phone call from Beau.

"Hello?"

"What do you mean you are handling this deal? We discussed this client as a joint call?" The irritation in Beau's voice is apparent.

"I need to do this myself. Since we have never discussed the client in full, and I set up the pitch meeting myself, I'm going to handle everything." I try to sound confident.

"You can't pitch this by yourself, Lucy. You know I can close this for you." His voice is rising.

"It's my deal, my client. Maybe we can team up again in the future," I say with little conviction.

"What is going on with you? You can't do this by yourself."

"I can, and I will do this myself. I'll call you later." I end the call before Beau can protest again.

I feel guilty for not including him in this deal, but I need to do this on my own. Has he always been such a bully?

I try to erase the entire conversation from my mind so I can focus on the client meeting I'm headed to now. Ok, think, Lucy: debt ratios, return on investment, balance sheet consequences.

My hands are clammy against the steering wheel as I turn into the downtown parking structure of my client's headquarters. You can do this, Lucy. You can do this. I'm so nervous, but excited too.

I did it, I did it! I can't believe I did it. I closed this deal 100% by myself. Every single detail was handled by me, and I nailed the deal before the meeting even ended. I was so scared and doubting myself, sure that I would mess up the presentation in some way.

I climb the five flights of stairs to my office with ease, the result of adrenaline pulsing in my veins. Swinging open the stairway door to our office, I confidently walk through the quiet cubicles. As I turn the corner toward my desk, I see Beau sitting in my chair. My body freezes.

I ease back around the corner and consider what I just saw. It looked as though Beau was rifling through my desk. Anger and fear displace the excitement of closing my deal.

An incoming text causes my phone to ding, the volume up so high the entire office could probably hear it. Fearing Beau will catch me hiding around the corner, I step out into the walkway and toward my desk. Beau observes me as I walk the last few steps to my cubicle.

"Where have you been? I thought we could work on the pitch for the Rural Valley deal together."

"I just came from their office where I made an affirmative sale," I say, pride emanating from my face.

"Why would you cut me out of this? I thought we were a good team," he says, still sitting in my chair, making no effort to move.

"I told you. I need to do this on my own. It's time I stepped up my game instead of relying on you to close my deals. I'm grateful for all your help, but I need this for me right now," I tell him.

"Whatever. You really think you can do this alone because you closed one tiny deal? Go ahead and try, but don't call me when you get stuck," he says with an arrogance I hadn't noticed before. Walking swiftly from my cubicle, he never looks back.

Dumping my purse in the bottom desk drawer, I hit the power button on my computer and try to relax as the software loads. The ring of an incoming text erupts from my phone.

Master: *Tonight, 8 p.m. Wear something attractive.*

Me: *Like what?*

Master: *Something that makes you feel sexy. No more questions.*

Me: *Yes, sir.*

Now what? I was looking forward to a quiet night at home or with Quinn. And why do I need to dress attractively? There is nothing I could wear that would help me look attractive. This alternative therapy is starting to annoy me.

I spend the rest of the day closing out my file for the Rural Valley deal, ordering financials and Dunn and Bradstreet reports for a few potential clients. The afternoon zooms by, given all the work I have to do. Thankfully, I set a reminder to leave work, or else I would have missed my appointment.

At home, I search through my closet for something attractive, but nothing I put on seems to look flattering or sexy. I settle for a black dress with an empire waist and a low neckline. I feel comfortable in it, and I love the soft touch of silk on my skin. Pairing the dress with my highest black stilettos, I feel a little more confident and hope my choice pleases The Master.

Chapter 11

Keegan

AFTER CHECKING IN WITH MY TEAM AND going over new information, we determine Lucy needs round-the-clock surveillance. We make a loose schedule to guarantee she is properly covered at all times of the day. The jailhouse chatter has increased, but we still have no firm details on the final plan or when it might occur. All we know for certain is there is an outside party with immediate access to Lucy and knowledge of her routines. The real mystery is why Lucy would be a target after all this time. Her kidnappers were tried and convicted, and no possible motive for retaliation against her can be determined, which makes the team extremely leery. It's like we are searching for one fleck of sand in the middle of the desert.

I take the night surveillance shift so I can watch Lucy while she is most vulnerable. This is dangerous territory for me, as I feel I am already too close to Lucy, but I know I can protect her. Formulating a plan, I send the text to Lucy telling her to meet at 8:00 tonight. Then I get my things together in preparation for the long night ahead.

I'm at the club early prepping the room for Lucy's arrival. Tonight, I will push Lucy further than planned. I need her to accept herself, to see with her own eyes how brave and beautiful she is.

I have noticed Lucy is extremely particular about her appearance, always wearing a professional but ordinary suit so as not to call attention to herself. Her makeup is more natural than not, but is always carefully applied. The only thing remarkable about her is her shoes. Her shoes are slightly higher heels than I would expect from her. I sense this is her way of rebelling, a way for her to feel sexy or confident.

Lucy is not fat, but I know she views herself that way. The cut of her suit does nothing to accentuate her lovely curves – curves that should be seen and not hidden. Everything about Lucy's life points to her lack of self-confidence. Her clothing, her job, her extremely limited social life. Her closest friends are all just like her, allowing each other to remain in their comfort zones.

I have only been watching Lucy for a week, but I'm seeing a subtle change in her demeanor. At our first session she did not look up from the floor once despite her curiosity. But at our last session, she looked me in the eye longer than I had anticipated. As a dominant, I do expect my submissive to do as ordered, but I was hoping Lucy would balk at my demands or try to quietly disobey my directives. However, she didn't budge. Quite possibly, she was not prepared for our meeting and retreated into a stable mentality of obedience. Our second encounter went much more as I had planned. Curiosity got the best of Lucy, and she looked me straight in the eyes. I also caught her checking out my body, which gets my mind working overtime.

I feel my cock twitch in my pants. Geez. Down, boy. It's not about you tonight. I try to distract my dick by going into the back room and calling my mom, but it doesn't seem to help. All that talk about the neighbor's prostate problems and the weekly happy hour tomorrow night does little to distract my dick from the beautiful woman who will be in my room before long. I agree to Sunday evening dinner at my parents' house and say goodbye. I open my locker and prepare for Lucy's arrival.

A chime in the prep room alerts me to Lucy's arrival. Ten minutes to show time. I finish changing. Then I turn on the undersized monitor that captures a small view of the room, mainly a view of the chaise and the wall behind it. I watch the monitor closely until Lucy finally appears on screen as she gets comfortable in the small chair just to the side of the sofa and chaise. The slow rise and fall of her chest is the only movement in the room. It's time.

The back door to the room is soundless, so I have the ability to enter the room without alerting my companion of my arrival. Lucy is sitting in the arm chair to the side of the sofa as instructed, facing the watercolor hanging on the wall.

"Stand and move to the center of the room, face the mirror in the corner," I command and watch as she complies with my instructions.

She is wearing a black dress, shorter than her normal work clothing, but not daring by most accounts. The dress is tight around the bust with a low collar that nicely accentuates her full breasts. The remainder of the dress falls straight, hiding all her glorious curves. Her feet are adorned with sparkly black stilettos. Her normally thick, dark waves have been straightened flat, falling delicately down her back. She has no idea how beautiful she is. I watch her look away from her reflection in the mirror. I knew she would have a difficult time looking at herself, so I leave her in front of the mirror for a few minutes. When I feel as though she has accepted her reflection in the mirror. I change direction.

I command her, "Turn around and face me." She does has instructed, like a good girl.

Standing facing each other, Lucy keeps her eyes low to avoid looking in my eyes.

I'm wearing a tight fitting black t-shirt, black coated jeans, and my mask. I watch patiently as she sporadically raises her eyes to study me. When I finally catch her looking at my face, she blushes and looks away from me.

"Look at my face, Lucy. Do not look away." She raises her eyes to mine, fear and curiosity flashing across her face. I slowly observe her body, starting with her legs and finishing with her eyes. A crease across her brow is the only clue to her fear, but I know she is scared. Standing before a man for the sole purpose of his pleasure is not something in Lucy's comfort zone.

I walk slowly toward her, continuing my visual assault of her body. When I am directly behind her, I observe her sculpted calves, no doubt from her evening walks up and down the hills in her neighborhood.

"Relax, Lucy. I'm merely enjoying your beautiful body, appreciating what you have presented to me. Tell me why you picked this dress?"

"It makes me feel sexy," she says delicately.

"But it hides your lovely curves."

"I don't have curves, I have fat," she says with conviction.

"Nonsense. I don't lie to my subjects. You have beautiful curves, full, perky breasts, and long, toned legs."

"Nobody has called me beautiful in years, and my family and old friends say I'm chubby," she testifies.

"They are wrong."

I take a few careful steps toward her. I turn her back around to face the mirror, putting my hands on her shoulders and massaging lightly. Moments later, I allow my fingers to lower the zipper on her dress several inches. I feel the lift of her chest as she takes in a deep breath. My cock is at half-mast despite my urging it to deflate. I see the short hairs on her arms standing at full attention, and goosebumps appear as well.

"I want to see you, Lucy, but I need your approval. Will you give it to me?"

Holding her hips gently, I feel her body tense at

my question. I allow her to collect her thoughts without intruding.

"Yes," she says quietly.

Before she can change her mind, I swiftly lower the rest of the zipper to just above her ass, then nudge the top of the dress gently from her shoulders. The silky fabric eases down her back and pools around her waist. I help the dress the rest of the way, and then it drops at her feet. Grabbing her hand, I encourage her to step out of the dress.

Standing before me is a beautiful creature decked out in a matching black lace bra and panty set. Clearly, Lucy had considered what might occur this evening.

I slowly walk around her, taking in every inch of her body. Her chest rises and falls with a heavy sigh, her eyes tilted toward the floor, her hands clasped together in front of her.

Bringing my hands to her hips, I ease her toward me until our bodies are touching, my front to her back. I know she can feel my hard dick resting firmly against her ass, yet she doesn't try to move away. Using both my hands, I collect her hair into a pony tail, then tilt her head back into my chest.

I allow my breath to wash over the side of her neck, while my other hand caresses across her stomach and hip. Moving my hand up, I place my palm over the thunderous beating of her heart.

I release her hair from my grasp, now needing both hands to explore her body. Her feet shift occasionally as I allow my fingers to graze across her skin. As I spin her back around to face me, I'm startled by the touch of her hand on my hip – grasping me as though I'm holding her steady.

Removing my hands from her body and stepping away, I command her to stand still. I walk quietly toward the back entrance of the room, willing my cock to settle down before I have to turn back toward Lucy.

Looking over my shoulder, I take in the beautiful girl standing before me. Fear and embarrassment frozen across her face.

"You are stunning, Lucy. If only you could see it as well."

I make the last few steps to the door and exit without another look behind me. I jog to the prep room where I grab my things and run toward the back door. I'm on duty to watch Lucy, and I need to be in place before she exits the building. I stuff my mask into my bag and pull on a clean t-shirt. Maneuvering my surveillance car around the building so I have a view of the office, I wait for Lucy to appear.

Chapter 12

Lucy

I'M STANDING IN A SEX CLUB, WEARING nothing but my underwear, allowing a man I don't know to touch me, ogle me. Confusion and excitement cloud my brain as I quickly step into my dress and pull up the zipper. Grabbing my purse, I beeline for the front door so I can get out of here and collect my thoughts.

I manage to get the powerless rental car onto the freeway rather quickly, the buzz of my phone annoying me as I bob and weave my way through traffic. As usual, I watch the lanes around me in the rearview mirror to determine if I'm being followed. It doesn't appear so, but I'm nervous and confused. I don't know why I'm allowing myself to continue with this crazy therapy. I have enough on my plate with my job and a stalker. I keep telling myself that I don't need this. Slowing off the freeway and into my neighbor-hood, I observe my neighbors' homes for anything unusu-al. Admittedly, I'm scared to go home. Scared of what may be waiting for me. The neighborhood is quiet, a few cou-ples who look familiar walking the streets. Pulling into my driveway, I peer into my yard and don't see anything con-cerning. I bolt from the car and jog to my back door, jam the key in the lock, quickly open, enter, and close the door behind me. I still, listening for the presence of an intruder, but I hear nothing but silence. Switching on the lights, I ex-hale deeply and try to compose myself. See, Lucy, nothing to worry about.

The vibration of my phone seems never-ending, so I pick it up to see what is happening. I have messages from Quinn, Beau, and Master.

I scroll quickly through the messages. Quinn is check-ing in to see if I arrived home safely. I respond that I'm home with the doors locked.

I check Beau's message next. He wanted to hang out again. Weird. That is two times he has asked to hang out at night – I get a weird feeling in my stomach but can't place the reason. Beau and I used to text all day and night, and lunch regularly. But it seems like in the last two weeks, we have grown apart. Maybe I've just been busy or something. I'm still mad at him for cutting me out of that deal, but whatever.

I tap the message from Master, and the butterflies flut-tering in my belly instantly travel south to my core.

Master: *I enjoyed watching you tonight.*

Master: *Your genuine innocence and stunning body are*

a refreshing visual.

Master: *Can I see you Saturday?*

I take a moment to consider his question before I respond.

Me: *I'm not sure I can continue.*

He responds instantly.

Master: *Are you afraid of me?*

Me: *No, not afraid*

Master: *Afraid of yourself?*

Me: *I don't know*

Master: *You do know, Lucy. Tell me.*

Me: *I don't know what I'm doing, why I'm doing this!*

Master: *Not good enough. Your body responded to me tonight, I want more. Tomorrow.*

Me: *No*

I don't know why I said no, but I feel like I need to slow this shit down.

Master: *How can I change your mind?*

I decide to ignore his message for the time being. It's Friday. I want to relax and put on my pajamas. I open Pandora on my phone and send it to the Bluetooth speakers in my house. The silence is now filled with low volume pop music – nothing too deep or heady.

I toss my clothes in the basket and remove pajamas from the dresser. I'm non-plussed and comfortable already. My stomach rumbles, so I check the kitchen cabinets and refrigerator, and sure enough, there is nothing to eat. With everything happening this week, I haven't had time to shop. I thrust open the drawer in my kitchen that houses a few take-out menus, pens, notepads, and various other items which don't have a proper home. I decide on Chinese, as they deliver, and order my favorite Honey Shrimp with candied walnuts, white rice on the side.

Luck is on my side, and I find a bottle of wine in the back of my fridge. Corking it swiftly, I grab a glass and fill it to the top with liquid comfort.

This is my typical Friday evening. A glass of wine and myself. I scroll through the media guide and look for a new series to watch. The doorbell rings. I grab my wallet and open the door without peering out the window. Keegan is standing there in the dark, smiling gently, the side of his face illuminated by the full moon overhead.

"What are you doing here?" I practically scream. "I thought you were the Chinese food delivery guy. You scared the shit out of me."

"I'm sorry, but I thought you would be more careful this late at night. You should never open the door, even for an expected delivery man," he says, as he barges into my house carrying two Chinese takeout bags.

"What are you doing here?" I ask again.

"I was getting Chinese takeout and the delivery driver is behind schedule. I heard the employees say your name, and I offered to bring your order to you," he says as though it's no big deal.

"Well, thanks, I guess," I say embarrassed, realizing I'm standing in my living room in my pajamas. I reach over to the sofa and grab the throw blanket, wrapping it around me.

"You brought my food. Thank you again. Now you can go," I say as I grab the doorknob to let Keegan out, but he has other plans.

"Nice place you have here," he says as he walks the short distance to my kitchen and begins unpacking dinner.

"What do you think you're doing?" I say in my most annoyed voice.

"Sorry. I just thought we could eat together since you are home, and I have no plans except to go home to an empty house. Do you mind?"

"Yes, I mind. I have things to do," I say confidently.

"Like what? You are in your pajamas, have removed your makeup, and are wearing those fuzzy socks girls seem to love. Looks like you are free to me," he says confidently while he opens my cabinets to collect plates and utensils.

"Nothing like inviting yourself in," I say, annoyed again.

"I'm sorry. Let's start again. Hi, Lucy. Would you like to have dinner together tonight?"

"If we are going to start over, don't you need to go outside and do it properly?"

"I'm not going outside, because I have a feeling you will lock the door, and I'll be stuck alone and without my dinner. I'm not going outside. Lucy, will you have dinner with me?"

"Fine, let's get this over with." Annoyance fills the room, which only causes Keegan to chuckle and stick his tongue out at me.

"What are you? Twelve?" I say, trying not to laugh.

He stares at me briefly, his eyes twinkle with gold tonight. "I have my moments," he says.

Grabbing some napkins and utensils, I make my way

to the sofa and set up a TV tray. Keegan sits down next to me, his leg gently touching mine while he leans forward to put down his drink.

A spark runs straight to my core. I squeeze my legs together, willing my desire to subside. The words "Down, girl" keep running through my mind. Why is Keegan here? Surely a hot guy like him has plenty of girls to hang out with on a Friday night.

"So really, what are you doing here?" I say without looking at him.

"I'm serious. I was getting takeout so I could go home and call it a night. I was waiting at the takeout counter, and I happened to hear them call your name for the driver. They had been arguing about how many deliveries needed to be made. So I stepped up and told them I was a friend and gave them your address, and they handed me your food. I knocked on your door, and here we are, eating, not alone. Win-win for both us of us, don't you think?" he says with that goofy smile on his face.

"Yeah, a real win-win," I say under my breath.

"What's that?" he asks.

"Oh, nothing." I take a big bite of shrimp and smile.

"Look, Lucy, you seem nice. I'd like to hang out with you sometime."

"Isn't that what we are doing now?"

"Well, yeah. What I mean to say is, I would like to take you out on a date."

"Oh…well." I'm speechless and can't think of a reason to say no.

"I'm not sure that is a good idea. I don't really know

you," I say, hopeful he will drop the subject.

"No better reason for us to go out then. To get to know each other better."

"Why? Why do you want to know me better?" I say, because really nobody other than my few friends have been interested in getting to me know in years, I think to myself.

"I thought I was being clear, but I guess I need to become Captain Obvious. Look, I think you are pretty, and something about you makes me smile. It's been a while since that has happened to me, and I'd like to get to know you better."

From the corner of my eye, I see him observing me. "Why?" I ask quietly.

"Why what? Why do I like you?" He looks at me in disbelief. I shrink farther into the sofa, clutching my dinner plate like a shield from his gaze.

"Do you really not know?" he asks me. Before I realize what is happening, his finger gently tilts up my chin so we are face to face. I want to look away, but his finger holds me still.

"I don't know what to say. You are a wonderful person and seem like a great friend. You have beautiful eyes, and a smile that lights up a room when you choose it to. A guy would be crazy not to get to know you, Lucy." His gaze never leaves mine, willing me to understand his statement.

When he releases my chin, I set my plate on the coffee table and turn toward him. As swiftly as before, he has my face in his hands, his cheek lightly touching mine, while he whispers in my ear, "How do you not know how beautiful you are?"

His head tilts back, and before I think of a good comeback, his lips are on mine. He locks me in a deep, gentle kiss, one hand caresses my shoulder while the other grips me by the waist.

I scoot back on the couch, then stand in horror that he may have touched the roll on my belly. Embarrassment shades my cheeks red, and I turn away from him. Tears threaten to fall from my eyes. The pounding in my skull matches the heavy beating of my heart.

I hear the rustling of Keegan's clothing behind me. I don't know what to do. His hands take hold of my waist, turning me to face him. I can't make myself look him in the eyes. He swiftly claims my mouth, the scruff of his beard teasing my face. The throbbing in my core returns with a vengeance when my breasts are crushed to his chest. For the first time in a long time, I allow someone to touch me, and I enjoy it.

Keegan

I won't let Lucy push me away for no reason. The feel of her returning my kiss, holding my pecs like they were her lifeline, sends blood rushing straight to my cock. I hold her close to me and urge my tongue into her mouth. Her response is reserved, yet wanting. My hand raises to her neck where my thumb caresses the line of her jaw. I feel her pull me closer. The sharp points of her nipples tease my chest through her thin pajamas. Braless. Just my luck. Her hands roam my chest while I raise the hem of my t-shirt until it is over my head. It drops to a pile on the floor.

My cock painfully throbs in my pants when I see the road rash on her face, courtesy of my short beard. Her small lips are now swollen plump, her hooded eyes sparkling, taking in every inch of my naked chest.

"Like what you see?" I question her confidently.

"Not bad," she says with a devilish grin.

She fingers the chain around my neck that holds my grandfather's wedding ring. "Does this mean something to you?" she asks me while inspecting the ring.

I pull her down onto the couch and hold her closely, her hand on my chest, fingers twirling my grandfather's chain.

"It was given to me by my grandmother when I entered law enforcement. My grandfather was a patrol officer most of his career then promoted to sergeant as he got older. My grandparents were already married when Gramps became a patrol officer, and he did not like the idea of removing his wedding ring to go to work. So my grandmother saved for months in order to purchase him a chain so he could wear his ring while on duty. She said that instead of wearing the ring on his finger, he could wear it over his heart. And he did just that, every day of duty until he retired. When he got older and forgetful, he wore it on the chain all the time. My grandmother hoped it would keep me safe as it did my grandfather. And so far, so good."

"What a delightful story! Your grandparents had a special kind of love you don't often find anymore," she says with a hint of despair.

I look at her innocent face, and a content smile waves across my mouth. "I would really love to keep kissing you to see where this goes, but I think this is far enough for tonight," I say. Then I stand and reach down to grab my t-shirt. Tugging it over my head and tucking my chain under the collar, I offer her my hand. She stands, and I bring her close to me, holding her tightly. Pulling away slightly, I lean in and give her a final kiss. A hint of a smile crosses her face as our lips connect. I enjoy this last taste of her before drawing back.

"I had a great time getting to you know you. I would like to do it again soon," I say as we shuffle toward the front door.

"I enjoyed getting to know you also," she says softly. Her cheeks blush slightly as I squeeze her hand then let go and turn for the street.

"Lock up," I say over my shoulder. I hear the door close followed by the thud of the dead bolt.

My cock is rock hard, throbbing incessantly, hoping for a release. I stroke it gently through my jeans hoping it will settle down, but nothing seems to help. I'm preparing for a bad case of blue balls tonight. I get into my truck and drive away. Joey has the surveillance duty tonight. I hope he didn't zoom in to my face while I left the house. Tonight did not turn out as I had planned, so I stop at his car and try and do damage control.

"What's up asshole?" I say as I pull up to Joey's surveillance car.

"Just your dick," he says, laughing hysterically.

"Nothing like that, bro. Just a little dinner, trying to get some information."

"What info did you get other than her bra size?" he squawks in my window.

"Dick. It's nothing like that." I shrug.

"Whatever, bro. Get out of here before you cause a scene."

I hit the gas without a goodbye. Maybe he bought my story, I don't know. I'm sure I will find out tomorrow at briefing. I drive home, shower, and rub one out. When I finally get into bed for the night, I lie awake thinking of Lucy's beautiful face and kick ass body.

Chapter 13

Lucy

I WAKE TO THE SOUND OF A LAWN MOWER IN
the distance. Glancing at the clock next to my bed, I'm
shocked to discover it's already 9 a.m. The chirp of my
phone in the next room coerces me from the warm comfort
of my bed. Pulling on a pair of fuzzy socks, I pad into the
kitchen to start the Keurig and check my messages.

12:04 a.m.

Beau: *you awake*

Beau: *call me in the morning*

1:35 a.m.

Master: *Sunday, 7pm. See you then*

7:55 a.m.

Quinn: *Coffee in 10?*

Quinn: *Call me later*

8:35 a.m.

Beau: *Brunch, 11 a.m., Morning Perk?*

I consider Beau's request. Things have seemed strained between us, so maybe this is a good opportunity to clear the air. Perhaps this is a white flag on his part. And besides, brunch at Morning Perk is too good to pass.

9:12 a.m.

Me: *11 a.m. Brunch...see you then.*

Next, I ponder the text from Master. After the events of last night, I'm not sure continuing with this therapy is appropriate or necessary. On the other hand, I haven't felt so alive in a long time. The emotion pulled from inside me has been startling, and I don't want it to fade. I make a mental note to discuss this with Andrea at my next appointment.

9:14 a.m.

Me: *7 p.m. Sunday, ok*

Then I respond to Quinn.

9:15 a.m.

Me: *brunch w/Beau at 11? Join us*

Quinn: *Pass, that guy is a tool*

Quinn: *call me later*

Me: *Luv you Quinney*

Quinn: *ok LuLu*

I scroll through my social media accounts looking for anything interesting or important. Selfies, political memes, and cute puppy videos don't interest me this morning, so I click off and jump in the shower. I enjoy the pounding of the warm water on my back, thoughts of Keegan and what happened last night weighing heavily on my mind. It has been so long since I have felt normal, since someone treated me as normal and not some broken little girl who would be beautiful if she lost forty pounds. I am tired of being the girl who is looked upon with pity because of her mental illness problems. I think of all the coping mechanisms, strategies, and sincere advice I have received from Andrea, and for once, I believe what she has told me. I genuinely feel maybe there is hope for me. Hope for a future I had relinquished long ago.

Maybe I am worthy of lust or even love. I'll take lust right now, because the feeling is completely foreign to me. I have erected a wall around myself so tall and menacing that no human dare scale it. And I can't agree that I'm willing to completely tear down that wall, but I'm ready to open a small door and see what comes through it. I consider sending Keegan a text letting him know that I enjoyed seeing him last night. But again, I have no idea what to do under the circumstances. Is it too early to text? Will I look desperate or needy? Everyone knows I'm desperate, but I don't want to make it seem worse than it is. Am I needy? Possibly. But I'm also human and have needs that have been pushed below the surface far longer than I ever imagined. Instead of pondering the issue to death, I decide to embrace the day as it comes and hope for the best.

Choosing a comfortable pair of skinny jeans and light tunic-style sweater with the phrase "Coffee Till Cocktails" emblazoned across the front, I flop into my rental car and drive to brunch. For the entire drive, I can taste on my tongue the delicious Mediterranean omelet filled with lush feta cheese and succulent tomatoes and topped with a remarkable dill cream sauce, paired with decadent, crisp rosemary potatoes. I may have agreed to brunch because of the omelet, but I am curious how this encounter will unfold. The drive allows me to consider what position I want to take with Beau. Am I willing to overlook him back-stabbing me and move on, or should I proceed with caution? Understanding the consequences of both positions, I decide to see how the conversation progresses.

Beau has secured a booth in the corner of the bustling family diner known for their house-made sauces and family recipes. He smiles when he sees me approach, standing to give me a friendly hug. It's like nothing has happened, and we pick up as the friends we normally are.

We talk about everything but work, which means Beau tells me of his latest conquest: the girl who will not give him the time of day, and his failure to understand why she doesn't want to go out with him.

"Seriously, maybe she has tool-dar," I say laughing.

"What is tool-dar?" Beau asks with a scowl.

"It's like radar, but for tools. Maybe she knows you are a player and doesn't want any part of that? A tool-dar. I know this will seem shocking to you, but have you considered she may not be attracted to you?" I ask flatly.

"Impossible," Beau responds indignantly.

"Time to up your game, player," I tell him.

Beau laughs. "At least I have game, Lucy."

"Touché."

We continue to discuss frivolous things before Beau brings up the elephant in the room.

"Look, Lucy, I'm sorry about the deal at work. I made a rash decision, and I should have called you or figured something out that didn't put you in a difficult position. While I will not apologize for making the sale, I will apologize for not trying harder to come to a mutual agreement."

I'm frankly shocked at his apology, rendered speechless.

"Your silence freaks me out because we both know you are rarely short on words."

"Sorry, I…Thank you for the apology. Let's just move on, ok?" I say earnestly.

"To moving on," he says, raising his coffee in the air. I clink mugs with him and take a sip.

Our conversation turns to me and what I have been doing. While Beau knows that something happened to me when I was younger, I have not made him privy to the details. I let it slip that strange things have been happening to me, beginning with the appearance of Mac Made Easy in my desk drawer. At first, he chuckles as though I'm joking. But when he notices I'm not laughing, his face straightens.

"Are you serious?" he asks.

"I know it seems odd to be concerned over a container of Mac Made Easy, but I have extremely unhappy memories of eating nothing but that faux food for weeks. And whoever placed it in my drawer must know that. What I don't know is why someone is doing this to me now or what the possible end game could be," I say defeated.

"Gosh, Lucy, I had no idea. Do you need to alert the authorities and security in our office building?"

"I have contacted the authorities, but no actual threats have been made, so there is little that can be done at this time. I keep telling myself it's all just a bad coincidence. Like maybe a coworker dropped that stuff in my drawer as a joke not knowing what happened to me. My contempt for powdered foods is no secret to anyone in the office," I say with a chuckle.

"Is that the only odd thing that has happened to you? What about your car accident? All this adds up to a strange collection of events. Where have you been this week? You have rarely responded to my texts as though you are busy. Is there anything else you haven't told me?"

"I did meet this guy, but I don't think he has anything to do with this," I say, hoping Beau doesn't press me for details.

"A guy? Since when do you meet guys? This looks all too convenient. A stalker, a car accident, meeting a mystery man at the exact same time all this occurs. What do you know about this guy? Where is he from? What does he want with you?" Suspicion drips from his words.

"What do you mean, 'What does he want from me?' You say that like it's unbelievable that a man might be interested in me," I say, anger rising from my throat.

"When was the last time a guy was interested in you, huh, Lucy? You can't tell me, and that is why all this seems suspicious." His voice is rising.

"I thought you were my friend, but here you are throwing me under the bus again. Friends support each other not tear each other down. This was a mistake," I say loudly, gathering my bag and standing before he can respond. I walk quickly out the door, leaving him with the bill.

I'm so fucking mad that the only thing I can say is fuck. Fuck this.

This shitty rental car is cramping my ability for a fast getaway. I see Beau running after me as I coax this clunker away from Morning Perk. Telling myself to relax, I conclude that a quiet afternoon at home is the best medicine for the situation. I decide to text Quinn when I get home and see if she wants to come hang out at my house. She is always good at distracting me from the destructive thoughts that invade my brain.

I arrive home, quickly closing the garage door and jogging to the back porch. I'm on high alert from the anger boiling in my veins, but I decide to get control of myself and take several deep breaths. This is just life. People come and go for better or worse. Sometimes it takes a long time to recognize that some friends are really anything but friends.

I open the fridge to grab a bottle of water and every relaxed molecule in my body disappears when I witness the foreign contents of my fridge. Breathing becomes difficult, the beating of my heart ceases, and I hear nothing around me but white noise.

Chapter 14

Keegan

WALKING DOWN THE STAIRS AT THE gym is a bit embarrassing. Apparently I went a little too crazy working my legs, particularly in the squat rack. It is not uncommon for this to happen to me during a challenging case. Thoughts of Lucy cloud my brain, rendering my judgement questionable. The only real method to clear my mind is to lift lots of weights, especially heavy weights. Hoping to ease some of the soreness from my workout, I hit the sauna for twenty minutes, followed by a quick steam shower. After cleaning up and changing, I make a beeline for the lounge to check my messages and put a plan together for the day – I really need to unpack the rest of my stuff, call my grandma, and do a boatload of laundry. As soon as my phone is powered up, it erupts in my hand with dozens of missed calls and text messages.

12:37 p.m.

Joey: *we got problems*

Joey: *call ASAP*

Murphy: *We have a situation. Call in for details*

Pressing Joey's contact number in my phone, I jog to the back of the gym parking lot where my truck is parked.

"Dude – where you been?" Joey hollers into the receiver.

"Pumping iron at the gym, what's going on with all the messages?" I ask loudly.

"There was an incident at Lucy's house."

"What? Is she ok? What's going on? Give me the details. I'm on my way now," I say as my truck's engine roars to life.

"It's curious for sure. Lucy was out to brunch with Beau Montgomery, according to her surveillance team, and everything was fine until she abruptly stormed out of the restaurant. No big deal. But when she returned home, there was an item planted in her house. She flew out of there like a bat out of hell. One of the team members stayed behind, while the other followed her to Quinn Sawyer's apartment. Our guy on the ground entered her house through the back door and ultimately discovered her refrigerator filled with EnsureLife. You know that shake-like drink given to people who are ill or elderly?"

"Yes, I know the drink," I say, annoyed. "What else."

"The surveillance team pulled up her case file and discovered that during her captivity, she was fed nothing but EnsureLife and Mac Made Easy. We are working our sources to see what message this could be sending."

"Yeah, this is an odd way to scare somebody, but it's obviously working," I say, baffled. "Where is she now?"

"At Quinn Sawyer's apartment. We reviewed the audio surveillance tapes from her house, but there is nothing to be gained except the sounds of the perpetrator packing her refrigerator."

"I'll call in to Murphy and see if he wants me on the clock," I say.

"The team is on it right now. There is nothing you can do at this point, but call him if you want."

"Keep me posted, bro," I mumble.

"No problem, dude," he says before disconnecting the call.

The desire to call or text Lucy is overwhelming, but I need to be careful. I'm wading into deep waters already, and I don't want to drown myself in the situation. I need to be clear-minded and formulate a plan before I reach out. I decide to text my boss, Murphy, to see if he has new information.

Me: *Any new leads in the Meadows case?*

Murphy: *Nothing worthwhile yet*

Me: *ok*

We know these incidents are related to the kidnapping from years ago, but we can't seem to connect the dots. The thought does not comfort me, nor does it help me keep my distance from my sweet Lucy. It's not like me to risk my career by seeking a relationship with her, but I can't get her out of my head. I replay in my mind the look on her face during our sessions when she starts to feel wanted, adored, admired. The rush of color to her cheeks, the sparkle in her eyes, the goosebumps that pop up across her arms – I want it all.

Better judgement aside, I decide to text Lucy. I want to protect her, and the best way to do that is having her with me as much as possible.

Me: *Hi there*

She replies within a minute, to my good fortune.

Lucy: *Hey*

Me: *What r u doing today?*

Lucy: *hanging out with a friend*

Me: dinner tonight?

Lucy: *Yes, I'm having dinner tonight.*

Not sure what she means by that, I decide to be as direct as possible.

Me: *Have dinner with me?*

Lucy: *Not sure I'm up to it*

Me: *Why*

Lucy: *just things*

Me: *Is everything ok?*

Lucy: *Let's not text about it*

Me: *Can I pick you up at 7?*

Lucy: *why*

Me: *I want to see your beautiful face*

Me: *hear your laughter*

Me: *put a smile on your face?*

Me: *Please*

Lucy: *I won't be at my house*

Me: *ok, where*

She gives me the address I know is Quinn Sawyer's

apartment then tells me to text her when I am out front. I feel deep down in the depths of my soul that this relationship will end badly, but I can't stay away from her, and I can't tell her the truth. Knowing that I need to keep busy for a few hours until I pick up Lucy, I decide to finally sort through the last few unpacked boxes in my condo and try to tidy up the place in case I have a visitor later.

Promptly at 7 p.m., I text Lucy from the front of the apartment building and wait at the bottom of the stairs for her to appear. The expression on her face is unreadable, possibly a mixture of fear and excitement. I reach for her hand and bring her in for a quick embrace.

"How are you?" I say, hopeful. Her lips upturn slightly at my remark as a faint blush rises in her cheeks.

"I'm ok, thank you," she says quietly.

"I was thinking sushi for dinner. Is that good with you?"

"Oh, well, I'm not really into sushi, but I can find something on the menu."

"I want to go somewhere you enjoy, so let's pick something else. Italian? Gastropub? Mexican?" I question.

"Oh, Mexican might be nice. There is that place near downtown that is supposed to be amazing, The Taco King," she says with a smile.

"Tacos it is."

I try to keep Lucy talking as we make the 20 minute drive, hoping to get her to relax. We talk about little things like the weather, the old homes we pass as we head into downtown, and the charm of the timeworn neighborhoods. It's funny to think about a city like Los Angeles as old when I have spent time on the East Coast in much older cities with more charm in their alleyways than you can find anywhere LA. But it's my home, and I see the original character of it all. Lucy talks about going downtown with her parents when she was a kid to the French dip place, and how it seemed such an adventure compared to her idyllic surroundings in the valley where she lived as a child.

Finding a parking spot on the street can be tough, so I navigate through the roads a few times and come up lucky with a spot just one block from the restaurant. Helping Lucy from the truck, I hold out my hand to her, and she takes it, but I see the hesitation in her eyes. My connection with Lucy is still on uneven ground, and I need to help her see she can trust me. I can't help but think what an asshole I am, believing Lucy should trust me when I am keeping secrets from her. My feelings for her are genuine, but I'm walking a slippery slope with my actions. Showing Lucy my true self, my feelings, my desires, is the only possible way to convince her that I'm genuine.

Opening the large wooden door to The Taco King, I watch Lucy as she enters the old church that now houses this *it* place for street tacos. Watching her admire the inside is a sight to behold, her eyes surveying the large beams crisscrossing the ceiling, studying the intricate scenes of the stained glass windows that cover the far wall of the building. She smiles when she catches me observing her. Again the bloom of rose coloring her cheeks makes my dick swell. The hostess waves us to follow her, and I'm grateful for the distraction as I follow Lucy to our table, adjusting my dick in my jeans, hoping to tame it into submission.

Our booth is located in the far corner of the main dining room which affords us an expansive view of the active space and the terrific architecture.

"The architecture and charm of this place is amazing," she tells me.

"It's pretty awesome," I agree.

We order margaritas, mine on the rocks. Lucy asks for hers blended with a splash of pomegranate.

"You didn't get a chance to tell me about the rest of your family. I'm sorry, did you say you have a sister?" she asks me.

"Yes, my sister, Kendra, is an elementary school teacher in the central valley. I haven't seen much of her the last few years, but we talk and text a lot. As far as brother-sister relationships go, I'm lucky. Kendra is a great sister and my biggest cheerleader. When I was considering moving to the east coast after college, she encouraged me to do it. She has always been the voice of reason in my life, other than my parents."

"What about you, any siblings?" I ask.

"I have a brother who is seven years older than me. We are friendly to each other, but our lives were so different that we never really bonded like you and your sister. He works for my dad. I think he wants to take over the business in a few years. JJ, my brother, is really outgoing, can sell anything with a great amount of ease, and has always been part of the *in* crowd. The exact opposite of me. While I had lots of friends growing up, I was still shy and more reserved than JJ. Due to our age difference, by the time I was eleven years old, he was out of the house, working for dad, and living in an apartment with his buddies, so I often felt like an only child. I'm not complaining. Compared to most people, I have a very good life, and I try to remain grateful to my parents for doing their best." Her eyes look away from mine, and I detect a hint of sadness in her posture.

"I know what you mean. My grandma used to tell me when I was a kid that no matter how bad I thought I had it, I would be more successful, attractive, loved, than 95% of the human population. She didn't say that to be smug. She wanted me to know how fortunate I was to grow up in California, to have loving parents, good health – all these things that come in limited quantities to the rest of the world," I say with pride.

"I get what your grandmother was saying. She seems like a sweet lady," she says with curiosity.

"Grandma is great. I try to have lunch with her once a week, but I get so busy with work, I feel like I miss our lunches more than I make them."

"I'm sure she is just grateful to see you."

We place our orders – Lucy gets two tacos a la carte. I get 6 tacos each with a different filling. We ask for fresh guacamole. Thank goodness they serve their guac fairly clean – just avocado, salt and pepper, and tomato. Living on the east coast for so many years has made me appreci- ate the purist style of guacamole prevalent in California. Guacamole should not be anything but avocados. I stopped ordering anything with avocado when I was living in DC because I never knew what was going to show up on my plate. The east coast version of guacamole frequently resem- bles nothing close to an avocado.

"How is your margarita?" I ask, noticing she has downed 2/3 of the glass.

"It's amazing! I love the pomegranate arils on top. This place is awesome. Thank you for bringing me."

"You're welcome. I'm just glad I was able to convince you to come out with me."

"I'm glad too. I admit I wanted to stay home and veg with my friend, Quinn, but thanks to you not taking no for an answer, and Quinn threatening to kick me out of her house if I didn't go, I'm here and having a good time as well," she says shyly.

"So what are you doing at Quinn's house?" I ask, hoping she will confide in me.

"A small issue came up at my house. It will be fixed and cleaned up in a couple days, so I'm staying with Quinn to keep out of the way of the workers."

The truth and a lie. Not terribly surprising. "Oh, no. What happened? Is it something I can help with?"

"It's just a small infestation of sorts. I have it under control, but thank you for the offer."

"I really have nothing planned tomorrow except dinner with my parents, so I'm free to help you. And I enjoy getting my hands dirty or picking up a hammer once in a while. Happy to fix whatever the problem, if possible." I watch her face change from content to annoyed, but I'm not backing down, not yet.

"Again, thank you, but I have everything handled," she says curtly. "Do you have dinner with your parents every Sunday, or is this a special occasion?" she questions, trying to change the subject.

"Not every Sunday, but we try to do it somewhat regularly. Since I returned to L.A., I try hard to see them every week."

"You have such a nice family," she croaks gently.

"Lucy, what's wrong?"

"Nothing, I'm sorry. I'm a mess. I love that you're close with your family. I don't have that, and I'll be honest, it hurts sometimes. My mom loves me, but she is just…different. We aren't terribly close, and since she got remarried a few years ago, she seems to be too busy with her new husband to spend time with me, except on my birthday or on other holidays you are supposed to spend with family. I'm not close with my dad, and my brother is fine, we just don't have a sibling connection," she recites quietly, like this is a speech she has given on several occasions.

"I'm sorry, I hate being a downer. Let's talk about something else."

Stunned into silence for the moment, I simply look at her face, realizing she won't lift her eyes to mine, as though she is embarrassed for confiding her feelings.

"You are far from a downer. I'm sorry that you feel that way. Sometimes we have to make our own families. Like I'm sure how you are with your friend, Quinn. It appears you two are close, like family," I say, hoping to lighten her mood.

"Quinn is a constant in my life, with no expectations about me physically or mentally."

"What physical expectations could anyone have for you?" Annoyance drips from my voice.

"My parents see me with this body and look at me with pity, as do many people I knew from a long time ago.

After high school, I was sick, if you will, and I gained a few pounds that don't seem to want to go away. Each time I see people from my past, they look at me as though I'm broken. I hear them whisper behind my back that I used to be so pretty and vibrant. And I would be lying if I said it doesn't still hurt my feelings."

"I can't imagine having any person like that in my life. Some people don't deserve you, Lucy. I hope you realize you are not what people think of you. Fuck them." She startles at my word choice.

"It's difficult when those people are your family. The only person in my family who never judges me is my grandmother, my only living grandparent. Unfortunately, she is getting up there in age, and her mind isn't like it used to be, but she is still with me and knows who I am."

"Fuck all those shitty people in your life. Look how amazing you are." Her eyes shoot upward to mine.

"There is nothing amazing about me. I'm just a girl trying to get by in life."

"Well, fuck that too. I'm not sure who you see in the mirror, but I'm looking a stunning girl with a heart of gold. You can be anything you want, Lucy. Don't forget that." She looks away, clearly embarrassed.

"Ok, enough talk about shitty people and feelings. What should we do next?" I ask.

"Let's go back to the valley and maybe hit up Old Town. It's only a block from Quinn's apartment."

"That sounds good. There are a few good bars over there, and I think they have a street fair every Saturday evening. Maybe we can catch the last hour of entertainment before it shuts down for the night," I say.

"That sounds great."

I pay the bill, leaving the billfold on the table, and we make our way outside for the short walk back to my truck. This part of downtown L.A. is busy on Saturday night, so it's not dangerous, but I take Lucy's hand in mine anyway. I feel her hesitate at first, but then her firm grasp warms my hand. I feel my dick twitching again. Lucy is not like any girl I have wanted in the past. I usually choose women who are brash, brave, and shallow. Dating shallow women is great because they are usually too absorbed in themselves to be bothered when I break up with them. I haven't desired a long term relationship in the past. I was too busy working, enjoying single life in DC and New York, to be strapped down to one woman. Clearly, I'm changing. Growing up, as my grandma would say. Because all I think about is being with Lucy, cherishing her, owning her.

I click the locks on the truck and pull the door open for Lucy. Before she can climb into my truck, I tug her gently to my body. As she starts to pull back, I take her face with my hand and lift her chin to me. My lips crash on hers with a gentle owning. The delicate touch of her hand to my chest signals my cock to raise. Deepening the kiss, I tease the seam of her lips with my tongue, and she opens gently, her tongue matching my caress. I pull her close to me with both hands on her hips. She wraps her hand around my neck, pressing her breasts into my body, caressing the hair at the nape of my neck. Before I am sporting a full erection, I break the kiss. Smiling, she opens her eyes to watch me.

"I would love to continue kissing you, Lucy, but

honestly, if we don't stop now, I won't stop anytime soon." She smiles deeply at my words.

"Thank you for tonight. I may forget to say that later, so I'll say it now, if that's ok?"

"You're welcome. Now hop in the truck." She climbs into my truck with ease. I jump in the driver's seat, and we set off for the valley.

Chapter 15

Lucy

I'M SO AWKWARD. I HAVE NO IDEA WHAT TO say while we drive back into the valley. Thankfully, Keegan is great at small talk and keeps us busy with light banter and some good tunes on the stereo. That amazing kiss runs on replay through my mind. It's been so long since I have had a kiss that shook me to the core. I feel the warmth between my legs spread through my body like wild fire. Keegan treats me normally, no remarks about being a nice girl or the girl with the pretty face and the chubby body. He makes me feel normal, wanted, and dare I say loved. Not loved, that can't be it. Maybe cherished. I feel cherished. A feeling I have never known.

Thankfully, we make it back to the valley rather quickly. My mind doesn't have enough time to run through all the doubts creeping up, to question why a handsome guy like Keegan would be interested in somebody like me. We park on a road adjacent to Main St. where the Saturday evening street fair is still taking place. The street is filled with vendors selling various items from handmade soaps to clothing and jewelry. A henna artist is tattooing a long line of customers, several local farmers are selling fresh vegetables and fruits, and there is a live band as well. Many of the shops on the street remain open for the fair and the large crowds. The smell of kettle corn and cinnamon bread lies heavy in the air.

Keegan takes my hand as we walk along checking out each booth. He points to a small pub and pulls me along as we pass by the stage for the live music. Classic rock blasts through my ears as I take a last look at the fair before we move inside the quaint pub. A small hi-top table for two is open near the front window, giving us a view of the sidewalk filled with people. The scene is like a dream - families walking together, children with ice cream cones, couples old and young holding hands. I try to accept the vision before me as ordinary. This is what normal people do, and I can be normal.

The pub happens to be a pouring location for several local breweries, so we choose from a large menu of beer. Keegan choses some IPA I have never heard of with Monster in the title. I ask for the BrewBerry – an amber ale with a touch of blueberry. Keegan makes a fake gagging noise at my choice, and I roll my eyes, not bothered by his teasing.

Conversation flows easily between us as we discuss meaningless things in our lives like music and cars.

"Look, Lucy, I would really like to help you fix whatever is wrong with your house," Keegan implores.

It's not that I don't trust Keegan, but I just don't know if it is wise to tell him about what is happening in my life. I fear I won't hear from him again. But I also know he has some job in law enforcement, so maybe he would not be scared away. I hear Andrea's voice in my head telling me to take a chance and confide in Keegan, that trusting people is a necessary part of life, and sometimes our trust in broken, but it is not healthy to keep everyone at arms' distance. I take a deep breath to prepare myself for the story I decide to tell Keegan.

"There isn't really anything to fix. I don't know how to explain what is going on, but somebody broke into my house, which as you can imagine has me scared. Quinn generously agreed to let me stay at her house for a few days until I relax a bit."

"I'm so sorry. Did they break a window or the locks on your door?" he asks, concern emanating from his body.

"No, nothing like that. It's difficult to talk about, but I may have some type of stalker. Odd things, mainly food, have been placed in my house and office, but I don't know who is doing it."

"That is strange. What do the police say? Surely they have dusted for finger prints and reviewed surveillance tapes from your office?

"Umm, the police have no evidence right now," I say, despondent. "It really could be nothing or just a practical joke, but I'm not taking a chance. So I'll stay with Quinn for a few days, and then I will be fine. I really don't want you to worry because really, this could all be nothing."

"This makes no sense, Lucy. Let me call your contact and get him working on your case. You can't live like this. It's not appropriate."

"Hey, thank you, but it's under control. I just felt like I should let you know, even if it turns out to be nothing."

"Well, please let me know if anything else occurs. Call me immediately so I can help you," Keegan pleads.

"I'm sure it's nothing. But thanks," I say, trying to encourage a meaningful smile from my lips.

I change the subject by asking Keegan about his truck. It's an easy conversation for us, and I know it will not lead into subject matter that I don't want to talk about – like my stalker.

"When will your Mustang be repaired? Have they given you an estimate?"

"Two more weeks, I think. I know all the parts have been ordered and the body work starts this week. I can't begin to tell you how much I loathe my rental car. I feel like a little old lady! I'm so scared to pull out into traffic because it has no get-up-and-go power, so I find myself waiting and waiting for a big enough opening where I won't get in anyone's way," I say laughing.

"That's no fun. I totally can't relate to your dilemma, even though my truck has a lot of power, it's definitely not a sports car. But because it's big, I can get away with almost anything on the road. I start to switch lanes and the entire freeway moves out of my way - wouldn't trade that feeling for anything," he says with a sexy laugh.

For the first time, in a long time, I feel normal. Like

going on a date is something ordinary for me, that I'm not this crazy, fat girl I see in the mirror. I look around the bar, and I don't see people staring at me with pity, or feel the eyes of strangers judging me with contempt. It's like I have finally outgrown the shadow cast over me by the past.

"Hey, Lucy, you ok?" he says, gently putting his large hand over mine.

"I'm great, sorry. Just enjoying the atmosphere. I haven't been to the street fair in ages. Tonight has been nice. Thanks again for convincing me to get out of the house."

"The pleasure is all mine," he says, then leans into my space and kisses my lips. Not one of those embarrassing PDA-type kisses that causes everyone around you to gag, but a sweet kiss. He starts to deepen the kiss then pulls away, leaving me wanting more. Opening my eyes, I see he is getting out his wallet to pay the bill.

"Are we done here?" I ask, confused. Not wanting the night to end, I get the feeling Keegan is trying to wind up the evening.

"Let's get out of here and see what else is going on. It's great weather to be outside. I feel like it's getting cramped in this place. Ok?" he asks me, signaling the waiter to take his card and the check.

"Sure, that sounds great," I say, trying to keep my composure. I'm not sure if this is a blow off, or if I'm poor at reading body language. Stop thinking, I tell myself. Not every movement, every action, has to have a reason.

The waiter returns the billfold, and Keegan signs the receipt, then replaces his card in his wallet. Catching me watching him, Keegan grabs my hand and encourages me off the bar stool. Before I can reach down to grab my purse, he has pulled me gently against his body and is kissing me as though he is taking his last breath. His lips are pressed tenderly against mine, but the grip of his hands signals his heavy desire, as he pulls me tighter to his chest, my breasts settling snugly against him. He ends the kiss, bends down to grab my bag, and hands it to me quietly. Placing his hand in mine, Keegan walks us out the door into the cool evening breeze. The sky above is clear, so the moon shines across the quiet street, casting a delicate glow.

"What now?" I dare to ask.

"It's getting late. How about I walk you home? It's such a beautiful night for a midnight stroll."

"That sounds nice." Walking west on the quiet side-walk toward Quinn's apartment building, we pass the time talking about Keegan's high school football career. He played running back on the varsity team for three years and holds the school's current record for most rushing yards in a single season. The homecoming game was a few weeks prior, and Keegan was invited to assist the offensive coach for the evening. Apparently, he keeps in touch with quite a few of his high school friends, which sounds amazing in my mind. After I was rescued from my abductors, my mother and I decided I would finish the last few months of high school via homeschooling. The school agreed and provided us with the coursework necessary to finish all my classes. I couldn't face my friends. I was embarrassed and destroyed by the incident, so I retreated from everyone. The ensuing years of depression and therapy allowed me to further re-move myself from my old life and friends. Keegan lives the life I always thought I would have. I dreamed of going to college, partying, finding myself. But all that changed in one night. Months later, I dreamed of waking up each day without the desire to die. I dreamed of wanting to live even if that life was lonely. Andrea usually reminds me that I made my dreams come true. I finally want to live. I wake up and don't think about going to sleep, never to wake up again. Getting to this point was hard, and I sacrificed my life, my everything, to survive.

I look up into Keegan's beautiful hazel eyes and congratulate myself for fighting, for not giving up on myself.

We approach the steps to Quinn's upstairs apartment, but Keegan stops short and turns around toward me. The reflection of the moon sparkles in his eyes. A warmth spreads from my core followed by the familiar flutter of butterflies in my stomach.

Thankfully, he doesn't mind initiating contact and pulls me close, taking possession of my mouth. Our tongues collide in a fevered frenzy. Pulling him closer to me, I press my breasts tighter against his body, wrapping my hands around the back of his neck. I feel his arm snake down my back as we deepen the kiss. As though he reads my mind, Keegan grabs my butt and pulls me into him, the thick, hard surprise of his erection now pulsing against my belly. Wanting to feel him in my hand, I move to rub him over the top of his jeans, but he pulls my hand away before I reach the goal and ends his possession of my mouth.

Opening my eyes, I see him watching me with hooded lids, cheeks flushed red with desire.

Keegan pulls me into a tight embrace and whispers in

my ear. "If I don't stop now, I won't stop until I have all of you. You have the most amazing kiss that drives me fucking crazy. I want all of you, Lucy. I want to feel my cock buried deep inside of you, the pulse of your orgasm strangling my dick. But not yet. Please understand how difficult it is to walk away from you tonight, but know we will be together when the time is right."

I pull back to look into his eyes and see nothing but hope and longing. The flood of my desire dampens my panties as I struggle to contain the ache in my core.

"I want you. All of you."

"You will have me, but I don't want to rush what is happening between us. We have all the time in the world for sex but only one chance for our first time." He kisses me deeply then retreats.

"Upstairs, wave to me from the window when you are safely inside with the door locked," he says over his shoulder, walking toward the sidewalk.

I jog up the stairs and let myself into Quinn's apartment and quietly move to the front window where I wave to Keegan. He gives me a short wave and then disappears around the hedge that lines the boundary of the property.

Standing in front of the window, I observe Quinn's neighborhood. I feel as though I'm being watched, but there is no movement outside. The light breeze rustles the branches on the trees, but otherwise nothing appears out of the ordinary. I'm sure it's just nerves from the situation at hand and adrenaline that remains from my date. As quietly as possible, I reach for the drapes and pull them closed, careful not to wake Quinn.

The rhythmic sound of water running in the shower wakes me from a restless sleep. I'm not sure if I can take another night sleeping on Quinn's sofa. I'm grateful to have a place to stay, but my back is definitely angry with the situation. Visions of my date with Keegan replay in my mind. Lying down last night, I wanted desperately to be with Keegan, but this morning I'm grateful that he wants to slow the pace of things between us. I don't trust myself and want to talk with Andrea about all the strange feelings I'm experiencing so I can be sure what I feel is real. The noise of my phone buzzing with text messages jolts me off the couch.

Master: *tonight, 8pm*

Conflicted, I decide to decline.

Me: *I'm done.*

Master: *Tonight will be our last session.*

Me: *Not a good idea*

Master: *I'm not asking. Tonight will complete our therapy, for now.*

Me: *Fine*

Master: *Fine, what?*

Me: *See you tonight, Master.*

Master: *Good girl. Until then.*

What am I doing? I can't deny that after the initial shock of our appointments, I feel different, I feel confident. I don't feel embarrassed about myself, my body, my shyness, as I have in the past. Having someone treat you like a delicate angel, something to be cherished, really helped me snap out of my mental stupor. Of course, I know that I'm not magically fixed, but this went a long way in helping me see myself from a different perspective.

Quinn comes out of the bathroom, a smile on her face like the cat who caught the mouse. I laugh because I know a grilling is forthcoming.

"We kissed and that's it. So get your mind of the gutter. Anyway, you know I slept on the couch last night, alone," I say.

"Tell me something else then. Is he a good or bad kisser? Because that has to be a make-or-break thing. There is nothing worse than a guy who is a terrible kisser. One of the guys who rams their tongue into your mouth with no finesse, like a lizard searching for bugs." She laughs.

"He's no lizard kisser, trust me. He's kind and considerate with me, but I feel power lurking underneath the surface. It was like he took possession of me. I definitely enjoyed it," I respond with anticipation.

"I'm glad you like him, LuLu. You look happy. Happier than I have ever seen." She crosses the kitchen to where I'm perched at the tiny bar separating the dining area and gives me a bear hug.

"Thanks, Quinney," I say honestly. "What do you have planned today? How about brunch and a chick flick at the theater?"

"Sounds good, Lulu. You get in the shower, and I'll check the movie times."

Chapter 16

Keegan

MY PARENTS EAT EARLY ON SUNDAY evenings which made it possible for me to set up a final appointment for Lucy later tonight. I want to firmly end our therapeutic relationship so I can move forward on a personal level with a clear conscience. Plus, I like to feel complete, that I performed with my subject in a manner that gives them closure.

I text Lucy because, let's face it, I'm becoming obsessed with making her happy, making her smile.

10:46 a.m.

Me: *I had a good time last night.*

Me: *Can I see you this week?*

Me: *Tuesday night, ramen?*

10:52 a.m.

Lucy: *Ramen shop, 7 p.m. Tues sounds great.*

Lucy: *I had a good time last night as well.*

I busy myself for the day doing laundry, planning my final meeting with Lucy, and doing a bunch of other menial tasks I've been ignoring.

Dinner with my parents was great as usual. It's so cliché, but mom's home cooked meals are greatly missed and appreciated. I can't recall the last time I had two days off in a row, but it's apparent from the stack of mail and laundry I cleared today that it was overdue. Maybe it's time I consider accepting investigations that don't completely consume my personal life as well. The long weeks have never bothered me in the past. I found it exciting and challenging, but the thought of regular hours sounds really appealing. I could have dinner with Lucy every Tuesday without interruption. Is it Lucy that is changing my mind about work? I decide to shelve the subject until the investigation into the threat against Lucy has been solved.

I climb the back stairs of the club and let myself into the office. Sundays are usually extremely quiet at the club, and tonight is no exception. In fact, the office is empty. I turn on the lights and unlock the front door so Lucy can enter without delay.

I prepare my room with extra care, then return to the prep area to wait for Lucy's arrival.

At two minutes after eight, the bell on the front door chimes, followed by the sound of a door closing in the distance. Checking the small camera to my room, I see that Lucy has followed the directions I left on the reception desk. I switch the camera to off and set my phone timer for ten minutes.

Soundlessly entering the room, I stay in the shadows to observe the scene before me. Lucy is standing in front of the full-length mirror dressed as instructed. Her soft curls swirl around her shoulders. The nude-colored lace bra and matching thong suit her understated style and fit her body like a glove. Hands at her sides, I watch her fingers rub each other, anxiety - or is it desire - playing with her emotions. The reflection in the mirror allows me to see a hint of her face, her eyes always cast to the side or the ground because she can't bear to see herself stripped down like this.

I take three steps into the room so we may begin. "Eyes on the mirror, Lucy." Her face lifts from the ground while her eyes search the reflection for a glimpse of me. She can't see me because I'm wearing a fitted long sleeve t-shirt, jeans, and the black mask she has come to know.

"Tell me why you look away from your reflection," I command, my voice maintaining a deep throaty pitch.

"I can't," she whispers. I walk further into the room until I'm steps behind her. She can see my reflection in the mirror as I observe her body. I take in her beauty from the top of her head to the tips of her toes, as though I have all the time in the world. I see her fingers continue to fidget as the weight of her body shifts from leg to leg.

"I see nothing but beauty before me. What do you see?"

"I see imperfections. I see why people look at me with pity. I see every mistake I've made, every regret." A single tear rolls down her cheek, but she makes no move to hide its appearance.

"You may turn away from the mirror and face me," I

command. She turns quickly in place so we are face-to-face, just steps away from each other.

My eyes rake over the front of her body as she watches. I'm fearful that she may finally recognize me, so I keep my eyes moving. Tonight I took extra precautions to disguise myself. My hair is slicked heavily with gel, and my usual V-neck t-shirt is replaced by a crew neck to hide any chance that she might see the tattoos covering my chest. Maybe it's the fear of being caught or the desire I have for Lucy, but I'm struggling to keep my dick under control.

I quickly step across the room to retrieve a bag of props I gathered for tonight then take my place standing behind her luscious body. Turning her around, I place my hands on her hips and guide her body to mine, my chest resting against her back.

"Don't think, Lucy. It's just me and you here. No judgements, no wayward looks. I will not allow something from your past to distort what is happening in this room. I am a man admiring a beautiful women – both your inner and outer beauty."

Starting at her hips, I run my hands along her body, across her belly, down to the tops of her thighs. Moving back upward, tracing the outline of her body with my fingertips, I feel her shiver under my touch. With one hand around her belly, I pull her tightly to my chest while the other hand works the clasp of her bra. Before she can protest, her bra releases from her back and is swept from her shoulders, falling to the ground in a puddle. My arm swiftly moves from her belly to grasp her across the chest, covering her full round breasts from the slight chill of the room. A quiet gasp releases from her mouth, her head tilts back onto my shoulder, followed by the points of her nipples hardening under my arm. I release her from my hold and step backward until we are no longer touching.

"Continue facing forward, arms at your side." I will my voice into the deepest baritone I can manage.

Pulling the large spool of raffia ribbon from the bag, I unwind enough so I can set the spool on the ground without it hanging. Placing the end of the ribbon across her breast, I take her hand in mine moving it to her breast, holding the ribbon end in place. I gently begin to circle her body wrapping her with every ounce of desire from deep within my soul.

Lucy

Maybe it's the combination of extreme desire and the ball of anxiety sitting in my belly, but my senses are on fire, hyper-sensitive to every movement, touch or word, stripped bare of my insecurities, and then wrapped in the warmth and desire found in the human touch. Closing my eyes, the intensity of his hands traveling across my body floods my core with desire. To my surprise, a moan escapes my lips. My eyes search for his but come up empty. He moves swiftly but gently around me then stops at my back, as I feel him secure the ribbon in place.

"Hold onto my shoulder and step into the remainder of your costume," he says quietly.

I look down to see a delicate red tutu placed at my feet. Gently touching his shoulder for support, I step into the center of the tutu. He slides the silky garment up my thighs and over my butt until it rests gently on my hips. I have never felt so adored, so wanted in my life. I don't even know this person, but he has awakened the real me that has been hiding below the surface for so long. I feel like a cherished possession, a princess, a queen on her pedestal.

"An angel on earth," he says quietly. "I hope you find your wings soon," he exclaims from across the room. The click of the door closing signals the end.

He is gone before the reality of what happened hits me. I slump onto the couch, pulling my legs close, rocking away the fear gripping my heart. Tears roll down my cheeks like a downpour across the parched desert. What has happened to me? I'm overcome with emotion that doesn't make sense. Am I mourning the end of this relationship, the loss of myself? Am I grieving for the life I have now left behind? I don't know. Concentrating on the music playing in the background, I try to take deep, slow breaths, willing my pounding heart to slow.

Chapter 17

Lucy

RECOVERING FROM MY FINAL SESSION LAST night took more than an hour. My emotions and senses were so heightened, I was afraid to even drive. Once I finally seemed to calm down, I changed back into my street clothes and drove straight home. I didn't think about it at the time, but going home by myself wasn't the best idea. Fortunately, there were no surprises waiting in my house, and I drifted to sleep quickly thanks to exhaustion of the day. It's a new week, a new chance for the life I deserve. I can do this on my own. At least that is what I'm telling myself during the drive to work.

Focus, Lucy, I keep telling myself. Each Monday, we meet with management to discuss leads, follow-ups, and any snags involving deals currently on the table. A planning session. This will be the first week where I will not have Beau as my partner. Dread begins to grow deep within me, but I shake it off as best I can and mentally try to plan my day. I'm also concerned about the direction my friendship with Beau has taken. We don't seem to be casual friends any longer. Each of our last encounters has ended badly. I need to come to grips with the reality that our friendship has run its course. Funny how life changes direction so quickly. A month ago, I dreamed of being with Beau, his strong alpha-style with women, his easy confidence. In my mind, he was the perfect man – a man I could never have - but my dream nonetheless. Now I can't imagine even being friends with him, his selfish and shallow tendencies so apparent.

I park in my usual spot on the lower level of the parking structure – it's always empty, so I get a spot close to the stairwell into the lobby. Without fail, I navigate the five flights of stairs to the floor where my office is located. The quiet hum of computers and office machines is a welcome sound as I put away my things and prepare for the day. My computer boots into startup mode just as Beau walks up to my desk.

"We need to talk. Can I get a few minutes before our sales meeting?" he asks.

"I don't think we need to discuss anything." My voice is unsteady.

"Please," he implores.

"Alright, give me a minute. I'll meet you in the conference room."

Beau nods in agreement and walks away quickly. It dawns on me that I really don't know him like I thought. I gather my things for the planning meeting just in case this discussion with Beau takes longer than I hope. I search my pencil drawer for one of the wayward stones that Andrea gives me from time to time. Not sure what the makeup of this round yellow stone will yield for me, I grab it anyway, hoping for a boost of confidence or clarity. The last thing I want is to go into this meeting unprepared. Talking with Beau is not high on my priority list, but I suppose we should get everything out in the open so we can move forward.

I walk into the conference room where Beau has taken a seat at the head of the table and close the door gently behind me.

"We need to talk about this guy you are seeing," he states abruptly.

"What? He's none of your business. What has gotten in to you?" I ask, appalled.

"Everything you told me yesterday makes no sense. The only thing that links all the events is this guy. A guy you happen to meet after you get in a wreck. A wreck that you won't tell me about because it probably bolsters my point. I know you can drive that car well. You didn't run off the road because you were going too fast. Something happened, and then magically this knight in shining armor shows up to rescue you. I bet you haven't even been to his house or know where he works. He keeps all that from you, doesn't he? Because he's hiding something. I think he is your stalker, or whatever you want to call it, and I don't want to see you get hurt." His voice booms across the room.

My mind is racing. Keeping my breathing even is a chore. What Beau just said rings true, but something in my gut tells me to trust Keegan. He told me about his grandfather's necklace, and we discussed his family – you can't make up those things, can you? But he abandoned me at the scene of the crash, he walked away. He later apologized for his actions – that can't be faked, can it? I know he is genuine, but I can't deny the curious timing of his appearance along with that of the stalker. My mind spins, considering everything I know about both these men. Beau may be arrogant and shallow, but he has always been honest. What do I really know about Keegan? Dread rises in my throat. The opening of the door snaps me back into reality until I look that direction.

"Who are you?" Beau demands.

"I'm here to end this, right now, Mr. Smith," Keegan announces to the room.

"I don't know a Mr. Smith. I'm going to call security." Beau reaches for the phone on the credenza behind him.

I'm left frozen in place, speechless, as I observe Keegan standing in the doorway. "Keegan, what are you doing here? Wait…" Then it dawns on me who he really is, FBI. I turn away from him, now looking toward Beau.

"You two know each other? Oh, now I get it. Mr. FBI is the guy you have been seeing," Beau says, his voice filled with amusement.

"That's enough, Mr. Smith. Security is a little busy at the moment, but feel free to give them a call if you must," says Keegan. "Beauregard Montgomery Smith, youngest child of Kyle and Jennifer Smith, brother to Grayson Aaron Smith, you are under arrest for the murder-for-hire of Lucy Meadows."

I feel the color leave my skin. The walls seems to close in around me. My breath becomes short, labored.

"Grayson. You are Grayson's brother? What is going on?" I manage to gasp between breaths.

"Come over here, Lucy, now," Keegan insists.

Suddenly, I'm ripped from my chair by the throat and dragged further into the conference room, the cold steel of a gun pressed to my temple. My vision becomes cloudy but I fight to resist it. Fear squeezes my lungs, but I manage a few shaky breaths.

Within seconds, a dozen men stream into the conference room surrounding Keegan. Their uniforms have all kinds of acronyms emblazoned across the front: FBI, SWAT, and LAPD. A man in a rumpled grey suit takes his place next to Keegan.

"It's over, Smith," the man in the suit announces. "We uncovered the little scheme cooked up with your brother. You won't come out of this room alive unless you release Lucy."

"I may as well be dead after what this bitch and her dad did to my family. Poor little Lucy, all fucked up from being kidnapped and left in her underwear for three weeks. What about my family? Lucy took away my entire family. There is nothing left but for her to pay for sending my family to prison." The sound of Beau's voice is foreign, as though he is a stranger.

A loud crack shatters the quiet of the room. Beau's grip on my throat eases as he falls to the ground. Huge men armed with all types of weapons descend on us, the sound of metal and leather stirring the fog left in my brain. The last thing I remember is being carried from the conference room, my hand gripping the citrine gemstone I had hidden in the small waist pocket of my skirt. My mind searches for protection, warmth, security, as my fingers grip the small stone.

Keegan

I carry Lucy from the conference room, but she doesn't recognize me as shock begins to overwhelm her. Her body relaxes in my arms as I rush toward the elevator. The doors open to reveal the paramedics that were staging downstairs. I lay her down gently on the stretcher. The medics help secure her as we make our way to the ground floor. Her face is unruffled, relaxed, and unaware of the chaos that surrounds us. Stepping off the elevator, I'm faced with my boss, who directs me to the side where a temporary command center has been constructed.

"Caldwell, you can't go with her. I'll send an agent to keep an eye on her, but that agent is not you. That going to be a problem?" he asks.

"No, sir. No, problem," I say hesitantly.

"Good. Good work. We still have lots to do here. Check with the lead agent upstairs who will handle the shooting investigation." The squawk of his com device interrupts my response.

"Smith stable and on the way down." It all happened so quickly. I don't know whether to be angry or happy that

Beau did not perish. The image in my mind of Lucy with a gun to her head heats my blood to boiling. I know he will be punished for his crimes, but will that be enough for Lucy? My dear, Lucy. I'm struck with the realization that she may awaken without me to hold her hand, to explain to her who I am, how much I want her, how I love the sweet smile on her face. Snapping myself back to reality, I hit the elevator button. The sooner I handle my part of the case, the sooner I can get to Lucy.

The day drags on as I try to wrap up my part of the investigation. As a member of the lead investigation team, I'm required to meet back at our office to go through the last bits of Beau's crime. I join the crew filling the conference room on our floor. We begin to work through the case, putting together a timeline of events and piecing that information together. My responsibility has been mainly surveillance and acquiring information from Lucy as to who may be part of the conspiracy. While I did not uncover any useful details, my colleagues certainly did. One by one, they go through the bits and pieces, creating a dialogue so twisted, I'm rendered speechless.

After the Smith family was arrested and tried for the kidnapping of Lucy Meadows, the youngest son was sent to live in a foster home on the other side of Los Angeles. That son, Beau Smith, allowed his resentment for the Meadows family to guide his every move. After completing high school, Beau went to a local state college where he earned a liberal arts degree in math. A natural salesman, Beau went on to study finance, setting his sights on landing a job with the bank that now employed Lucy. Hoping to destroy any happiness in Lucy's life, Beau befriended her, gaining her trust. There are gaps in his story, but maybe he will fill those in for us in the coming days. We believe his goal was to destroy her career, destroy her life, little by little, until she had nothing left. Somewhere along the line, the plot turned into a murder-for-hire, the payoff being Lucy's multi-million dollar life insurance policy.

The forensic accountant in our office had been doing some research trying to find a link between Lucy or Beau Smith and the off-shore LLC that purchased the life insurance policy. After several weeks of digging through records across the US, the team finally uncovered a classified listing for a tiny company announcing its legal business name. With a stroke of luck, our accountant recalled that company from a financial records listing he had been researching due to a possible link with this offshore LLC. The companies are related, shrouded in multiple name changes and business addresses. The owner – John Meadows. Lucy's father.

My heart breaks for Lucy. I don't want to finish reading the report but know that if I'm going to help Lucy, I need to understand the entirety of the deception.

A financial trail from Lucy's father, John, to the offshore LLC was uncovered. The team involved had difficulty finding a motive, which is imperative in any case where a trial may be on the horizon. Motive is necessary to understand the ultimate end goal of a crime. After more digging, the team uncovered a financial mess of epic proportions all leading back to Meadows Insurance. John Meadows' insurance business had been declining over the last 10 years – even before Lucy's kidnapping. In order to maintain his comfortable lifestyle, John organized numerous methods of cheating his clients by charging undisclosed broker fees and inflating premiums. It turns out that since the trial of Lucy's kidnappers, John had become increasingly sloppy when it came to hiding his illegal activities. The team is still in the early stages of researching and uncovering the depth of the fraud committed, but initial estimates by the forensic accountants suggest the fraud will hit more than several million dollars.

Flipping forward in the file to more about the Smith brothers, I learn that Beau's initial plan was to destroy Lucy's career and keep her fearful of strangers. The brothers wanted Lucy mentally tormented so heavily that her life would be limited drastically. Seeing Lucy's life fall apart, her mental illness exacerbated, and her failure to become successful were the ultimate goals. Once again, they wanted to exploit her psychological weaknesses, just as Grayson had done by stripping Lucy to nothing but her underwear during her captivity. Their desire to manipulate her life by distorting her view of herself turned out to be successful. Lucy had lived in a delicate state of fear because of her limited success as an investment associate. The team has asked for the cooperation of Lucy's employer in determining how deep Beau went to dismantle any success she may have garnered.

The final portion of the case book is the most disturbing and may be the straw that breaks Lucy's back, or it will be the closure she needs to move forward from all the difficulties in her life. During the investigation into John Meadows, a link was found between the Smith brothers and Meadows Insurance. While looking into the recent visitors for Grayson Smith, we discovered that John Meadows had a jailhouse meeting with Smith. The FBI arranged to view all of Grayson's jailhouse records where it was found that John Meadows made a direct deposit into his commissary account. From there, the trail went cold between the Smith brothers and Meadows, until we got word from the prison informants regarding the murder-for-hire plot.

My head pounds at the depth of this violation. I close the file, not wanting to know more. My partner, Joey, startles me from his desk across the aisle in our bullpen-style office.

"All cleared for the night. We can go home," he tells me matter-of-factly.

I punch the off button on my computer, mutter my goodbye to Joey, and then make my way to the parking lot to collect my truck. The hospital where Lucy was taken for evaluation is about half an hour from my office. I use the time to consider how I will explain the situation, how I will get her to understand. Fuck that. I'll make her see that I'm real. That every feeling I had, every touch was real. Is real. I don't pretend that it will all work out that easily, but I try to stay positive. Lucy has just suffered one of the most profound deceptions possible at the hands of her father, so moving forward will be challenging. But I'm willing to help her try.

Chapter 18

Lucy

MY MIND IS NUMBED BY THE information that has been relayed. I know I am in a state of shock both physically and mentally. The hospital told me I'm fine and is preparing my release papers. I called Andrea to see if she could come to the hospital and pick me up and counsel me in regards to the whole situation, but she is not picking up her phone. I'm sure she has patients the rest of the day. So I called Quinn, the most constant person in my life, to pick me up and deliver me home. My stalkers are in jail, so at least I can go back to my home and feel safe.

Dread creeps into my throat at the thought of having to contact my boss, Mr. Lewis, and ask for a few sick days. The events of the morning run through my mind in slow motion. The disruption the incident must have caused all my co-workers and the office shames me from the inside out. Why me? Why am I such an easy target? I keep to myself, don't cause problems, and the list goes on. I feel as though the FBI has not given me the entire story. Maybe I don't want to know the whole story. I'm so confused – I wish Quinn would get here soon. The door creaks as it opens, and I peer toward the other side of the room expecting Quinn, but it's not her. A few quick steps and Keegan is at my side, reaching for my hand, words coming from his mouth that I don't hear.

"Get out. Please. Just leave me alone," I say, defeated, tilting my body back toward the window, watching the clouds roll through the bright afternoon sky.

"I'm not leaving until you let me explain. Until you listen to what I have to say," he says adamantly.

I peer at him briefly without saying a word. I see the glint of gold peeking out from the collar of his shirt. To keep him safe while working, his grandmother told him. I wonder if that was all a lie. I don't want to care, but I'm hopeless, and I do care. I continue with the silent treatment, hoping he will give up and leave.

"I'm not leaving, Lucy. I hope you will listen to what I have to say," he says, expelling a deep breath.

"It's true I was assigned to follow you regarding this whole mess. The first night I was following you was the night of the accident. I saw the car run into the rear of your car forcing you into the concrete pillar. I wasn't supposed to reveal myself to you in the beginning. This was supposed to be a blind surveillance, meaning I wouldn't have contact with you. But my mistake turned into my fortune. I showed up to the hospital to collect you, against the wishes of our team command – I thought for sure I was going to get reprimanded, but I haven't yet." A nervous laugh escapes his lips.

"Everything I told you about myself is true. Every emotion I felt was real. We were real. I don't know what I could have done differently. I'm sure I could conjure up a million possible scenarios. But the truth is, I wanted to protect you. I wanted to find out who was stalking you, and I wasn't willing to risk telling you the truth and having you push me away or causing our investigation to become public. I expect you to be mad at me. But remember this - you are finally free. There was a third party involved in your kidnapping and stalking, and that person has been arrested and will be tried for his crimes. I don't know how much you have been told, but I would not change any decision I made. You can be mad at me, but you aren't going to push me away," he says with conviction.

Keegan's statement confirms that I haven't been given the entire story, so I decide to pressure him for details. I let him stand in uncomfortable silence for a few minutes while I collect my thoughts.

"You mentioned a third party? I haven't heard those details. I want the entire story. No bullshit, no sugar coating, just the truth," I say resolutely.

"Can we talk about that fact another day? Anything else, I'm an open book."

"All the information now, or you can get out. I'm tired of all the omissions and lies," I say unwaveringly.

"All right. Let me give you a really simplified account.

Please allow me to just get this out quickly. Anything that doesn't make sense, you can ask about when I'm done. Deal?" he asks.

"Ok."

"Beau on his own cooked up this scheme to make you pay for what happened to his family. You were the weakest link in your family's chain, so he went after you. He wanted to make your life miserable. He planned his entire life around making you miserable. Over time, he revealed his plan to his brother, Grayson. Simple revenge eventually turned into a murder-for-hire. The brothers contacted this third party in an attempt to extort money in exchange for scrapping the murder plans. It turns out the third party then took out an insurance policy on your life, hoping the brothers would get angry and follow through with the murder plan. Fortunately, we uncovered the identity of the third party and certain financial records that allowed us to link the three of them in the plot. Now here we are," he says, releasing a deep breath.

"This just doesn't make sense. Who is this third party?" I ask in frustration.

"Someone you know, Lucy," he says hesitantly.

"Who? Tell me now," I implore.

"John Meadows," he whispers.

The weight of the world once again comes crashing down on my shoulders. My father. My dad hoped to gain from my death. He wanted to benefit from my death. I feel tears running down my cheeks, puddling onto the collar of my shirt. I want to scream like a hysterical mad person, but I'm shockingly calm despite the downpour of tears. Maybe

I'm in shock again. Wait…no. No. He can't be involved, I think to myself.

"What else are you not telling me?" I say pointedly to Keegan.

"We believe your father was involved in your initial kidnapping, but we are still working all the leads in that regard. It appears your father's business has been declining over the last decade. Our theory is he cheated his clients by charging them illegal premiums for policies that were terribly inadequate. He would, in turn, pocket the difference in monies between what he charged his clients and the premiums paid to the insurance companies. The scheme came to light when the Smiths' business went up in flames, and they threatened to go to the authorities. From there, we can only guess what happened, but we believe your father was in on the kidnapping, hoping to recover funds for both himself and the Smith family from the Kidnap and Ransom policy he had purchased.

Most recently, the Smith brothers approached your father attempting to extort money in exchange for your safety. Your father double-crossed those guys in hope that he could collect from the insurance policy after you were killed."

My heart breaks once again. Broken by my own father. I know we are not close, but I have never hated my father. He has treated me badly because of the depression that has consumed my life since the kidnapping, but I never hated him. Now, I don't know. I'm confused, broken.

Thankfully, Quinn barges into the room saving me from having to be alone with Keegan.

"Thank you, Officer Caldwell," I say with little

conviction in my voice.

"It's actually Special Agent Caldwell," he says.

I stare at him. Did he really just correct me?

"It appears your work is done here. Goodbye," I say, then turn to Quinn. "My papers are signed. Let's get out of here, Quinney. Can we go home?" I ask her quietly.

"Of course, LuLu. I'm here," she says, pulling me into a quick hug. I get up off the bed ready to leave when Keegan grabs my arm stopping my forward movement.

"We aren't done talking this through." He looks directly in my eyes, his grip on my arm unyielding.

"I'm done. It's time for me to go home, and you're not going to make a fuss. The last thing I need right now is to hear more of your bullshit. Now let go of my arm," I say through gritted teeth with all the politeness I can muster. He releases my arm but leaves me with some choice parting words.

"I'm not done with you, Lucy. You have been through hell today, and I respect your need to calm down or accept the situation or whatever you need right now. But we are not done talking. I will be in touch soon," he says, then turns and walks out of the room in front of me and Quinn.

"What's his deal?" Quinn asks. She hasn't heard the whole sordid tale, but I'm too tired to fill her in, so I shrug my shoulders and start walking out of my room, then the hospital.

While Quinn drives us to my house, I rummage through my purse in search of lip balm, but instead I find a stone. I pull it out and gasp. Rarely do I recall the names or composition of the rocks that Andrea gives to me periodically, but I remember this one. Blue Lace Agate is one of my favorite stones because it has these blue and white waves or bands around the rock. They look like the calm waves of the ocean on a tranquil day. I hold the stone in my hand. My lips turn up at the corners in a semi-secret smile as I hear Andrea's voice in my head, "Blue Lace Agate is a stone of encouragement and support. It aids in promoting positive attitude and emotion." I'm destroyed by the news I received today, but grateful that I'm alive and physically unscathed. The next weeks will be tough, but I'm going to make it. For the first time in a long time, I know I will be ok, that my life work out regardless of what occurred today.

Chapter 19

Keegan

THE NEXT FEW DAYS ARE FILLED WITH compiling reports and sifting through mountains of data and evidence collected by the team. While the case has been solved, we aren't ready to close the file just yet. A few members of the team continue to search for financial records related to John Meadows and the large scale fraud he committed against his clients. Lucy's brother has claimed no knowledge of the deceit, and initial reports show all the fraud has been related to the John Meadows personal book of clients. Each agent in the office maintained his own book of business, so it's likely that no other agents in the office were co-conspirators in the fraud. The team has been congratulated with solving the mystery and uncovering this far-reaching fraud. My time on this case is coming to a close. The financial fraud case has been handed over to a team of forensic accountants with experience in solving this type of scam.

I walked out of Lucy's hospital room one week ago, hopeful that we could move forward from my deception. A few days later, I tried texting her, but my messages would not send. I wanted to have someone in our technology department check into her whereabouts using the GPS signal from her phone, but I decided against it. Moving forward, I need to treat her with faith and compassion. To gain her trust, she has to know I won't abuse my special access to government resources when it comes to our relationship. I wanted to send my partner, Joey, by her house to check on her, but that seemed like a dick move. She asked me for time, and I'm going to give it to her. Last night, I relented and drove by her house after work, hoping I might catch a glimpse of her working in her small garden or see her silhouette in the picture window of her living room. The house looked cold and dark, no lights illuminating the interior or exterior.

This whole wanting one woman thing has forced me into unfamiliar territory. I like to think I'm a modern man, but I want to grab Lucy and shake some sense into her, make her see that everything I kept from her was to safeguard her life. I want to overpower her and make her see that I will be good for her, that we have a chance at something amazing. But I also know that Lucy has to be in a fragile state right now, and telling her what to do is not going to go over well.

Closing the book on another day, I give my grandmother a call to see if I can take her dinner tonight. She is glad to hear from me and tells me to come over – only if I have Chinese take-out. Grateful for the distraction from my thoughts, I plan an evening out with my favorite person who can hopefully help me find some answers regarding Lucy. Grandma always knows best, and I really need her help tonight. I pray she tells me what I want to hear.

Chapter 20

Lucy

WHILE DRIVING HOME FROM THE hospital, Quinn and I decide that I need a vacation and that she would be more than happy to accompany me. I love her. She knows exactly what I need and how I'm feeling. We called to have a pizza delivered and spent the evening at my house searching through vacation rental ads throughout California. Hours of searching ended with us choosing a tiny guest house in beautiful Coronado, located just south of San Diego. It is a garage apartment with one bedroom, which we both agreed would be Quinn's so she could also use it as an office for work. The pullout sofa was just fine with me. We rented the apartment for a month, but Quinn agreed to only stay for two weeks, then I would have two weeks on my own.

I was given a two month leave of absence from my job to recuperate from the trauma that is my life. I'm grateful my employer was so understanding. They even gave me two of those weeks as paid leave. This is the first time since high school that I'm free to be me without worrying about living another day, paying my bills, finishing college so I can pay my bills, making all those dreaded sales calls so I can keep my job and pay my bills. It's like a never ending wash cycle. Just when you think the spin cycle is over, it starts again.

Fall weather on Coronado is nothing short of paradise. Clear blue skies and crisp morning chill, followed by warm afternoon sun. The apartment is walking distance from the main street and just three blocks from the ocean. If I'm really bold or energetic, I walk the width of the island to the bay and watch boats come and go from the harbor. I smile thinking about sitting in the bay park under the warm rays of the sun, watching the Navy servicemen on the docks across the bay tending to their ships. It has been such a simple and pleasurable time for me despite the events that led me here.

My father was arrested the same day I was held at gunpoint by Beau. It turns out the man I always wanted to impress was in fact a cheat. He stole money from hard-working families and business owners. All that time I spent crying that I wasn't good enough for him was for nothing. The success he proudly bragged about was nothing more than a distortion of his true self. He wove a lie so complex, he believed the truth would never be uncovered. How he treated me through my kidnapping and subsequent recovery caused me to see myself in a manner so distorted that I became a different person.

I have been talking with Andrea every few days to try and understand this whole mess. I decided that I wanted to concentrate on myself and not focus on the fraud my father perpetrated. I will never understand his reasoning for these crimes, and I will not spend another minute of my life concerning myself with him. Andrea is worred that this is just an avoidance technique – avoiding digging into our father/daughter relationship. But I assure her that there is nothing to avoid. We did not have a fruitful or loving relationship, so every minute I spend talking about it is another minute of my life wasted at his hands.

The last seven years I have spent hiding from life, people, family, and friends. For the first time ever, I feel confident and powerful. I know I have a lot of work to do on myself, but I'm excited for the future, whether good or bad.

Walking along the ocean's edge with sand between my toes, I decide to end my time in Coronado and return to my home. There are many loose ends that need to be tied up back home in the valley, and the sooner I handle it, the better. Plus, I got a call today that my precious Mustang is finally repaired and ready for pick up. I can't wait to get rid of this rental, to feel the vibration of the Mustang's engine rattle my bones. I spend my last day in Coronado walking downtown, going into my favorite shops, stocking up on little things to remind me of my time here: shell-shaped soaps, locally crafted olive oil, and a new pair of flip flops. I lay awake in bed with the windows open under the chill of the evening breeze, listening to the crashing waves in the distance. I'm alone but never feel lonely. I finally feel free.

Keegan

It's been weeks since I last saw Lucy that day in the hospital. After a week of driving past her house and seeing that she has clearly left the area, I decide to talk with Quinn. I knock on her door late one afternoon and ask her to have a cup of coffee with me. She meets me at the coffee shop around the corner from her home a bit later, and I plead my case to her. Quinn informs me that Lucy is doing well, and that when she's ready to talk, she will find me. I tell her I can't wait any longer, but she just laughs and finishes her coffee. The conversation was comforting. Knowing that Lucy is working on herself and is doing well makes me happy. But I won't be satisfied until I see her once again.

I decide to text her and arrange a meeting with my alter ego, Master. To my shock and surprise, she agrees to meet at the club tonight at 7 p.m. I really hadn't expected Lucy to agree, but now that she has, I need to get my mind together, come up with a plan of attack. Master needs to crumble what's left of the walls she has raised to guard her heart. I know in my soul that my alter ego, and me, can finally raise Lucy from the black hole she fears so desperately. After Master has completed today's task, I will make her see that she is mine. I'm done letting her keep me at a distance, I gave her space as she requested, but I'm done with that shit.

Of course, I'm anxious and impatient, so I drive to the gym for a quick one hour session with a bunch of heavy weights. The push and pull of using free weights helps release the tension running throughout my body. I finish up with a few minutes in the sauna before hitting the showers and preparing for my rendezvous with Lucy.

Chapter 21

I MAKE MYSELF COMFORTABLE AND TRY TO regulate my breathing as I wait for Lucy to appear. Why am I such a pussy – scared to meet a girl? I'm becoming soft and ladylike, but fuck it - if it means I get Lucy, then I will gladly give up my man card. Well, maybe not, but whatever. The longer I sit here, the higher my balls travel into my throat. I try to relax my mind and body with deep, focused breaths, but nothing seems to be working.

Finally, Lucy appears. My heart throbs with desire and my cock swells at the sight of her sweet face. She looks stunning in a simple red dress, silver stilettos covered in crystals adorning her feet. Her skin is slightly tanned, and her hair hangs around her shoulders. I walk into the room and command her not to turn toward me.

"Eyes forward," I say confidently. Lucy doesn't move,

but I see her fingers rub each other gently, a nervous tic. I close the gap between us but stop before we are touching, my chest to her back. With my mask firmly in place, I gently take her arm, turning her around to face me.

"I've missed you Lucy," I say, trying to keep the sound of my voice as deep as possible. "You look stunning and rested." I reach around her waist drawing her closer to me, her hands find their natural place on my chest. Before I realize my mistake, Lucy has pulled my chain from beneath my shirt. Seconds pass in silence, my eyes avoiding hers. Fear races through my veins. I feel the grip of her fingers around my grandfather's ring, so I take a chance and allow my eyes to find hers.

I'm overcome with emotion as I see a smile spread across her face. She gently removes the mask from my face, messing up my hair in the process. I quickly laugh at the stupidity of worrying about my hair and run my hand through it.

"I'm glad it was you," she says quietly, her eyes searching mine for acceptance.

"When did you know?" I ask hesitantly.

"Not until a minute ago. I saw the necklace near the collar of your shirt, and I wanted to touch it. When your grandfather's ring ended up in my hand, I instantly knew it was you. I'm glad it was you. I felt a connection to you the minute you walked into the room tonight. I wanted to see the ring on the end of your chain. I wanted you," she says while tears gently slide down her cheeks. I raise my hands to her face to wipe them away.

"Happy tears, I hope?"

"Definitely happy tears," she says, smiling.

"I'm so sorry for everything. I wanted to tell you about me, but I couldn't. I was afraid you would hate me, but I also wanted to protect you, to make sure you were safe until we figured out this whole mess," I say before kissing both her cheeks. I feel her hands at my waist as she tugs me closer. I wrap my arms around her shoulders pulling her as close to me as possible.

"Keegan?" she whispers hesitantly in my ear.

"Yes, babe, what is it?"

"Can you put your mask back on, and…you know…do your thing?" I pull away slightly so I can look down into her eyes. I see happiness, desire, hope.

"I'll do anything to be with you, Lucy," I implore. "Now turn around and face the wall," I say with every fiber of my being. She turns gently, giving me her back. I gently tug the zipper down the back of her dress. Coaxing the dress from her shoulders, it falls to the ground in a puddle of brilliant red. I give her my hand so she can step out of the dress. She stands before me in the sexiest lace thong I have ever seen and those tall, fuck me heels. I notice her shoulders lean forward slightly as though trying to shield her naked breasts.

I stand in front of her and pull my shirt over my head, my grandfather's ring landing with a thud against my chest. Lucy starts to step forward, but I command her to stop.

"Have you forgotten the rules?" I say. "You will not move or speak without my permission. I promise you are safe with me Lucy. Tell me your safe word."

"Gumball," she says, giggling.

"I prefer the banana gumballs. How about you?" I ask.

"I love banana, so rich and smooth and long," she says, like the devil made her do it.

"We will get to that, but not yet." I take her mouth in mine, claiming her with my tongue. I feel her hands travel across my chest and up to my neck. I lean down and grab the back of her thighs just below her ass, then hoist her up onto my waist. I feel her legs cross behind me. She kisses me like the world is ending while I walk us to the couch in the center of the room. I lay her down gently then allow my body to cover hers.

My cock throbs when it finds her warm center through my pants, aching to be freed from confinement. I nudge her legs open with my knee then lean down to take her light pink nipple into my mouth, the peaks already hard and pointed with desire. She moans at the intrusion, her body arching into mine, begging for more.

I feel her fingers gently release the button of my jeans followed by her hands pushing the waistband over my ass. I'm lost in her body, the feel of her skin against mine, the desire in her eyes beneath her fluttering lashes. I pull back and sit on my knees admiring the view beneath me. I urge her lacy thong over her butt and down her legs before tossing it into the growing pile on the floor.

"Your pussy is as beautiful as I imagined," I say while pushing my pants the remaining inches down my thighs. I'm lost, completely lost in her. She strokes my cock through my boxers then violently pulls them down my body causing my cock to bounce against her pussy. I kick the offending boxers from my leg and return to my place on top of her. My hand grazes the outside of her pussy, coming away wet with her desire. Taking her nipple into my mouth once again, I allow my hand to explore the folds of her now dripping pussy, my fingers gently parting her slit. Inserting one finger inside her steaming hot pussy forces a drip of pre-cum out the tip of my cock. I watch her face for signs of discomfort or fear but see nothing except desire.

Lucy

He gently slides another finger into my pussy preparing me for his cock. I reach down and grip his cock gently with my hand – it stiffens into a column of steel.

"I want you, Keegan. I want you inside me. Please," I gasp between breaths as his hand works my pussy into a frenzy. I grip his cock harder to get his attention, stroking his rigid length as best I can since my hand does not reach around his girth. He lowers himself to my mouth, dotting my face and neck with delicate kisses. When he nears my mouth, I pull his lips closer and devour him like cake on my birthday. Our tongues dance together in increasing harmony.

"Please, Keegan. I need you," I beg.

Grabbing his jeans from the floor, he extracts a condom, ripping the package open with his teeth. I watch as he slowly slides the protection over his throbbing member. He shifts his body onto the weight of one arm and grabs his cock with the other. Slowly he runs the head of his member through my slick folds. My back arches involuntarily, searching for a cure to the desire shooting through my core. I feel the crown of his cock breach my entrance, causing me to gasp at the slight discomfort.

"Lucy, look at me. Are you ok?" he whispers in my ear.

I open my eyes and nod. A smile crosses my face as I take in this beautiful man. His green eyes are the calm to my storm.

"I'll be fine. You are just big, and I haven't done this in a while, so I'm tight," I say, blushing.

He pulls out of me, then presses his head back in a little further this time, rocking in and out of me slowly and gently. The discomfort subsides as he continues to move in and out of my pussy, not fully seated. I wrap my legs around his back and rock against his cock in rhythm with his movements.

"Fuck me, please. It's so good."

He plunges his dick gently into me until his balls smack my ass. I wince for the final time as my pussy fully adjusts to the intrusion of his thick cock. He kisses me gently and forcefully as he allows my body to adjust then begins to prod again, increasing his speed when I urge him on with my legs and body. We find a rhythm somewhere between making love and fucking.

"Your pussy is so fucking hot, so fucking tight. It's like you were made for me," he says before he places my ankles on either side of his shoulder, then stills. At this angle, his cock is buried deeper inside me causing him to slow his rhythm.

"Look at me, Lucy. Watch while I love you," he whispers.

Once again, he begins rocking in and out of my pussy with increasing frequency. His thumb moves to where we are joined and begins to work my clit. Sparks shoot through my core. My head thrusts back into the pillow as I scream, "So good. Yes!"

Thrusting into my pussy with more intensity, he works my clit harder, coaxing an orgasm from deep within my soul.

Opening my eyes, I see him watching my face as his cock disappears inside me. I feel comfortable, like I'm finally home.

Fireworks shoot from my pussy as my orgasm seizes every muscle in my body. My back arches, my legs like a vice, squeezing every part of him until my orgasm recedes. Keegan pumps into me quickly and releases his seed, grunts of pleasure uttered from his lips. When his orgasm subsides, he lays the full weight of his body on top of me. I wrap my legs around his back and enjoy the feel of his body on mine. We lay in silence as our breathing returns to normal and his cock softens inside me. I hold his head with my hand, rubbing my thumb along the nape of his neck. I feel tears threatening my eyes.

"Baby, what's wrong? Did I hurt you, what is it? Tell me," he implores.

"I'm so good. I'm happy. Happy tears I guess. It has been an emotional few months, but I think I'm finally getting better," I say with hope in my heart. His cock falls out of me as he leans to the side removing his weight from on top of me. Pulling me closer, he holds me as close to him as possible, his hand running gently along my back.

I nuzzle my face into the crook of his neck, enjoying his fresh scent.

"What cologne do you wear? I love the smell," I ask him quietly.

"I don't wear cologne. It's my deodorant," he chuckles. "I could stay here all night with you," he says squeezing my butt cheek. "But I want to be home with you, make you breakfast, rub your feet, or whatever. Let's get out of here," he commands.

He releases my body from his grip. We separate to find our clothes. Keegan walks to the small en suite bathroom and disposes of his condom. We dress, watching each other intently. We leave through the front door, Keegan locking it behind us. He walks along with me to my car.

"Hey, you got your car back," he says.

"I picked it up today. I'm so happy to have it back! I hated that stupid rental," I say triumphantly.

"Let's get you home. Don't try any of your *Fast and Furious* driving this time, ok?" he shouts over his shoulder as he jogs to his truck in the far corner of the parking lot.

The drive home is uneventful. I check my rearview mirror frequently, not to look for stalkers, but to admire that big truck following me and the handsome man driving it. The realization that he wants me makes me both fearful and wonderfully happy.

I pull into the garage of my little house and finally feel at home. I have always loved my little bungalow, but something about it feels different. I feel like I really belong here. Maybe Keegan and I aren't meant to be, or maybe we are. Either way, I'm looking forward to feeling desire, love, and hope again.

Keegan's truck looks awesome in my driveway. I watch his form fitting t-shirt strain over his muscles as he walks toward me.

"Let's go home, babe," he says, taking my hand in his.

The End

Epilogue

One year later

Lucy

IHAVE BEEN WORKING FOR *GRAYCEFUL LIFE*, an online lifestyle retailer, for almost 6 months, and the excitement and happiness I find in working there is astonishing. Going to work every day is an adventure instead of a disappointment. Returning to my banking job was difficult, I'll admit. I gave it my best effort but realized I would never enjoy working in the banking industry. So I started looking for another job. To my surprise, a friend from grade school, Winslow, built an online retailer from scratch, and she just happened to be looking for a Brand Manager. I admitted to her that while I studied marketing in college, I was in no way up to speed in this field. She told me she thought I was brave, that I could manage anything I set my mind to, and we could take the job slowly until I got comfortable. I had overcome so much adversity in life, getting acquainted with the industry was going to be a piece of cake for me. Winslow was willing to take a chance on me, had faith in my abilities and aptitude, and gave me the job, no questions asked.

I have poured my heart and soul into getting to know her business and the market. Sure, I need to contact potential retail and lifestyle partners, but I don't find it to be challenging. Maybe I have grown up recently. Maybe loving your career makes anything possible. I still keep gumballs in my desk drawer and still make chewed gum volcanos, because some things should never change. Plus, I don't have to wear those boring suits any longer. I donated every single skirt suit in my closet to a women's job support organization. I've never been so happy to give away my clothes. The real bonus in my new life is that some days I even get to work from home in my favorite pajamas.

My life is blessed. Keegan moved into my bungalow a few months ago. We hardly noticed the difference in our living situation because he was spending most of his free time there anyway. I love taking my evening walk and seeing his truck in the driveway of our home. I'm still a bit of a homebody, but Keegan brings out the best in me. I'm getting better at loving and accepting myself, my appearance, my flaws.

I'm still seeing my therapist, Andrea, but I'm down to therapy once every other week instead of twice a week. All the work we put in trying to piece me back together over the years has allowed me to become a better version of myself.

A year ago, I would have never imagined the life I have to-day. Honestly, fear still clings to my soul once in a while. When I am overcome with emotions, I grab the small bag of stones I keep in my purse. They help remind me where I have been and where I'm going.

Acknowledgments

I imagine this will always be the most difficult part to write of any book. First, I would like to thank my husband, Matt, for his support during this process and his endless work providing for our little family. This book would not be finished but for the support of my greatest cheerleaders: Jenny, Jen, Leanne, Lisa M, JoAnn, Holly, Mary, Terrie, Melissa, Carrie, Ann and Christina. Your faith in me is mind boggling – I'll get the next round at Happy Hour?

Thank you to my book besties: Author Kacey Shea, Rikki, Tana and Amy for your unwavering support, too many great laughs and lots of amazing book chats.

Model/Actor Shane Williams challenged me to write this book, so he was the only choice to grace the cover and I can't be more pleased with the results – he makes a great Keegan!! Thank you, Shane, for taking Pokémon pictures with me, and of course, your kind words of encouragement.

The Furious Fotog himself, Golden Czermak, for taking this great cover photo and for his first class professionalism.

Sarah Hansen at Okay Creations for making my cover vision a reality on a very short timetable.

My editor and childhood friend, Lisa Murray, your patience and thorough examination of my manuscript are so appreciated. I can't imagine how many times you screamed at your computer while trying to grasp the poor state of my grammar. I'm grateful you don't get paid per comma, otherwise I would be broke.

Thank you to all my friends, family and readers for supporting my debut novel. As a writer I have my shortcomings, but I hope you follow along on my journey, as I grow as a story teller, thought provoker and most importantly, a human.

Follow Me:

Facebook: www.facebook.com/Melodyjonesbooks
Website: www.melodyjonesbooks.com